Blathers said, "Sure, they say that scallywag Hitler wants to take over all of Europe."

"Time will tell." I didn't want to discuss politics with Blathers at this point.

We went on a little farther, toward what we call the Flushing Entrance at the southeast end of the site. We could walk back to the office from there. "Behind this building here is where our jail will be."

We turned the corner to see how construction was progressing. Blathers said, "Faith now, what's that bundle o' rags in the corner over there." We looked closer. Blathers pushed the bundle with his foot. It didn't move. "Mother Mary be with us, it's a body."

"Holy cow, where'd that come from?"

We each looked over the body, an old man. It looked like he had been beaten to death and dumped there.

I said, "I need to get to Whalen about this. You stay here and make sure no one disturbs anything."

Dawn of a New Day

by

Michael B. Coyle

Dawn of a New Day

Cover Art by *The Wild Rose Press, Inc.*

The Wild Rose Press, Inc.
PO Box 708
Adams Basin, NY 14410-0708
Visit us at www.thewildrosepress.com

Publishing History
First Edition, 2021
Trade Paperback ISBN 978-1-5092-3607-7
Digital ISBN 978-1-5092-3608-4

Published in the United States of America

Dedication

For Kathe,
who keeps me writing

Book One: "A Pound of Flesh"
Chapter 1

He didn't fool me with the three-piece suit and fedora. He was as Irish as Paddy's pig, as they say. He could have been just off the boat. He wasn't very tall, maybe 5'10" in a stretch. Even though he seemed to be in his mid-twenties, his hair was almost pure white, parted in the middle. Perhaps it looked even whiter because of his ruddy complexion. He put his hat on the corner of my desk. "I saw your ad in the *Mirror*. Sure, it sounds like just the thing for me, doesn't it." His brogue was so thick you could cut it with a knife.

I said, "Tell me about yourself. How long have you been over here, lad?"

"Two years, now." He stopped talking.

"And what have you been doing for the last two years? Have you been working?"

"I have been." He stopped again. It was like pulling teeth.

"And, what were you working at?"

"Sure, I got on the police, but I didn't like it, did I."

"What was wrong with the police? Don't most of you Irish lads end up on the police, or the fire department?"

"Faith, and isn't that the truth. But, like my sainted mother, I don't like the politicians. Oh, I know being in politics has done a lot of good for the folks what have come from the old country, but I'm from a part of

Ireland where we aren't good at joining things. Sure, I could be walking a beat, taking home a good paycheck, and going out with the boys every Saturday night, but that's not me, is it. I didn't want to join the Democrats. I didn't want to join the Blackthorn society, and I didn't want to join the Hibernians. All that them fellows want to do is fight—fight in bars, fight in the street, and fight in Ireland. I'm here in this country because I'm tired of fighting."

Well, at last I was getting somewhere. "Did you have much of the police training?"

"I did some, and in the old country me father and grandfather did work as private investigators. They often worked with the local constabulary. I would help out. Even as a young lad I did some investigating from time to time."

Holy cow, I was afraid once he got started talking he wouldn't stop. "Well, I think you might be just right for this job. What is your name, man?"

'I'm Blathers. I have a first name, but for some reason, all the men in our family are just called Blathers. And you, sir, are?"

"My name is Duff."

"Duff is it. Me old granddad used to say a fellow was dry as duff if he didn't take a drink now and then. You're not a teetotaler, are you?"

I laughed. "I'm afraid I am. But that's okay. It leaves more for other folks to drink. By the way, I seem to have heard your name somewhere before, but for the life of me, I can't remember where or when." I shook my head trying to recall where I'd heard "Blathers" before, but it wouldn't come to me. I said, "Well, never mind, you can start tomorrow. Fill out these papers and bring them with you. You can read and write, can't you?"

"And sure, I can. I'll be glad to take the job. The pay is what the ad said, is it not?"

"It is. I'll see you right here at eight o'clock in the morning."

Chapter 2

My office was rented space on Main Street in Flushing, on the second floor, above a burger joint. The Long Island Rail Road rumbled by about thirty yards south, and the last stop on the IRT line was just down the street to the north. The place was convenient, close to transportation, burgers on the main floor, and close to home. I had an apartment on 41st Avenue, just around the corner.

The site of the Fair was only one subway stop away, at Willets Point. I was not on the site because the Fair wasn't open yet. I was interviewing people for security positions after the opening. My granddad and my father were private detectives, and like a chip off the old block, I joined their agency when I graduated from high school. Granddad had since gone on to his eternal reward, and Dad was working only part-time. It had been tough, what with the Depression and all; there had been hardly enough work to support Dad. I saw this job, head of security for the World's Fair, as an opportunity for the short term. My plan was to head back to Chicago when the Fair closed.

I was finishing my tea when Blathers showed up. "Good morning, Mr. Duff."

"Just call me Duff. It goes better if I'm going to call you Blathers. Have you had any breakfast?"

"Sure, I have. There's one of them little doughnut

shops in Grand Central. I got a coffee, doughnut, and orange drink for a nickel. Me sainted mother would think it a grand breakfast for the cost."

"I'm sure she would. Well, now then, lad, sit down, and I'll fill you in on the whole picture. You're the first person I've hired, so at least for now, you're my right-hand man. The Fair is set to open in six months, and we'll be hiring quite a few fellows. An event like this draws all sorts of grifters, pickpockets, and the like. Folks attending the Fair will expect to have a good time without being victims."

Blathers nodded and said, "Sure, and the way things are in Europe, political trouble will be a problem too, don't you think?"

"It may be. By the way, speaking of politics, did you know the man in charge of the Fair is Grover Whalen? He was once head of the police. You didn't have a problem with him, did you?"

"Ah, gee whiz, I do know Mr. Whalen, and I don't like the way he does business. But don't worry. Mr. Whalen won't be bothering either you or me. That's all I'll say."

Chapter 3

I thought the best way to start with Blathers would be to tour the site. The IRT line ran from Grand Central Station to Flushing. We took it one stop toward the city to Willets Point. I told Blathers, "This will be the entrance most people will use. Coming from the city they will probably get the IRT at Grand Central and get off here. Coming from Long Island they can take the Long Island Rail Road North Shore line and get off right over there. Most of the parking will be over here too. Even with the hard times, lots of folks on Long Island have cars. When the cons and pickpockets show up, the pros will use a less busy entrance, but the amateurs will come in here. We'll have people at all entrances. When we catch an amateur, we'll let him or her—there are plenty of women in the con games nowadays—anyway we'll just give them a warning, and suggest they move to the West Coast and try their luck at the San Francisco Fair. If we catch them a second time, we throw them in the lockup with the pros."

Blathers said, "Where is the hoosegow, then?"

"I'll show you. It isn't anywhere anyone can see it. We'll have a bunch of cells. The troublemakers will have a very uncomfortable night while we hold them before taking them to court the next morning. Now let's take a look at the layout."

We walked toward the centerpiece of the whole

show. "There's the Trylon and the Perisphere. They're almost done. They'll be the only white buildings at the fair. Folks will go through them and then go down that long ramp to enjoy the rest of what's going on."

"Faith, where in the world did they get the names Trylon and Perisphere?"

"I think they just made them up. They're supposed to mean something, but nobody really cares what they mean."

We walked around the buildings. Blathers said, "Sure, and aren't there going to be a great lot o' stiff necks from people staring up at these things."

"Yeah, but you won't get one because you'll be watching for the guy that's got his hand in the pocket of the guy looking up."

"Pickpockets will be our biggest problem, then?"

"No, but it will be one of the first problems. There will be some small-time and some big-time cons here too. Folks that aren't used to big city life will be coming to see 'the world of tomorrow,' like all the advertising calls it. The sharpies will jump on them like it's last call in a pub on Saturday night."

We were now in the Court of Peace. On each side the nations of the world that were attending the Fair had an area where they flew their flags. Blathers was, of course, interested in where Ireland would be, but he also asked if Germany would be participating in the fair.

I said, "That's a funny thing. No one will say if they weren't asked, or if they decided on their own not to come. I saw one story in the *Mirror* that said they were going to come but decided not to because of the money. The reporter had the opinion they would rather spend the money on weapons of war."

Blathers said, "Sure, they say that scallywag Hitler wants to take over all of Europe."

"Time will tell." I didn't want to discuss politics with Blathers at this point.

We went on a little farther, toward what we call the Flushing Entrance at the southeast end of the site. We could walk back to the office from there. "Behind this building here is where our jail will be."

We turned the corner to see how construction was progressing. Blathers said, "Faith now, what's that bundle o' rags in the corner over there." We looked closer. Blathers pushed the bundle with his foot. It didn't move. "Mother Mary be with us, it's a body."

"Holy cow, where'd that come from?"

We each looked over the body, an old man. It looked like he had been beaten to death and dumped there.

I said, "I need to get to Whalen about this. You stay here and make sure no one disturbs anything."

Chapter 4

I practically ran back to the office. I plopped in the chair and phoned the head office of the Fair in Manhattan. "I need to speak to Mr. Whalen right away. This is an emergency."

I had good luck. "This is Whalen. Who is this?"

"Mr. Whalen, It's Duff, out here in Flushing."

"What is it, Duff? Is there a problem? Is it something you can't handle?"

"Mr. Whalen, we've just discovered a dead body at the site. We don't know who he is, but it looks like he was beaten to death, right there on the premises."

There was silence on the other end of the line. I waited for the boss to say something. Finally, "You said we. Who else is we?"

"My new assistant, Blathers. He is standing guard at the site now."

"A young fellow just here from Ireland, a year or two? Parts his hair in the middle?"

"Yeah, that's him."

"Why did you hire him?"

"He seemed like a good man. He had some experience, and he felt you would find him acceptable."

"Right, right, he is acceptable. Now about the body, we will want to keep this as quiet as possible. Notify the police in Flushing. Have them call me, and wait until you hear from me."

"I sat back in the chair and phoned the Flushing precinct. Then I went back to the site and told Blathers, "We're off the hook for the time being. By the way, Mr. Whalen said he knew you, but he didn't sound so sure about you at first. Then he suddenly changed his mind. Do you have something on him that I should know about?"

"Faith, all I know is me father said I should look him up when I got to New York. I went to his office and sent in me name. His secretary came out o' the office with a note for me to take to the police. Before I knew it, I had a uniform and a pay envelope. I wrote to me father, and he replied that I need not worry. That's all I know."

I wondered, Is that all he knows?

Chapter 5

We waited. We stood. We paced. The conversation was limited. I told Blathers it was useless for us to speculate about who the guy was. We were sure it was a guy. We saw that much.

I made one good guess. "If he was on the site, he must have been working there. The general contractor is providing security during construction, but I checked them out, and their security is damn tight."

Blathers said, "But we walked right in. Nobody stopped us."

"That's because you were with me. You must have noticed there was a guard at the gate when we went in."

"I did see him."

"That's right. But what you didn't see was at least three other security people around dressed as workmen. They all know me, of course. Most of them are freelancers, and want me to hire them for the Fair. We'll have to find out why this murder, and murder it is, happened right under their noses. It didn't take us long to find the body. Why didn't those guys on the job find it?"

Then the Flushing cops arrived, and we went back to the office.

****

We continued to talk about the murder; it certainly was murder. We discussed the fact that Whalen seemed to want us out of the picture. Blathers sat staring at the ceiling, stroking his chin. I came to know that was his pose when he was deep in thought. As I got to know him better, I discovered that although he was not often deep in thought, when he was, it was wise to let him think. Eventually, he put his head down and said, "Sure, if Mr. Whalen wants to keep this quiet, and even if some of the current security folks aren't in on it, someone is going to get away with murder."

Finally the phone rang. "Duff, Whalen here. We've got the site all cleaned up. You have nothing to worry about. It appears to have been an unfortunate accident. Just keep on doing what you're doing. And, above all, don't talk to the newspapers. Leave all that to me. I'm experienced in that area, you know. Goodbye." Now it was clear. Whalen did not want us involved.

I said to Blathers, "Guess what. It was just an unfortunate accident."

Blathers stroked his chin again and looked at the ceiling again, but only for a split second. "Sure, I may be not long off the boat, but I know when I've seen a fellow beaten to death. And I don't like the idea of letting it go for any reason. Me sainted mother would say that this is a matter needs investigating."

Chapter 6

We found the body on a Friday. The weekend, Monday, and Tuesday passed. We didn't hear another thing about the unfortunate accident. Then about midmorning on Wednesday, a raggedy-looking fellow came through the office door. Blathers and I had been busy trying to decide how many and what kind of men we would need when the Fair opened. We were a little concerned that, if we hired any of the contractor's bunch, we might get some bad apples. There was also a discussion about whether we should hire people who looked like security guys, you know, the bouncer type, or folks who just looked like other folks and would blend in with the crowd. Blathers thought we might need some women, too.

The guy who just came in was one that looked like he could be one to blend in with the crowd. He was a skinny little fellow. He had chin whiskers, but they were as thin as he was. His thick glasses made his eyes look like they were way too big for his head, which, by the way, was topped by the same type of thin hair that was on his chin. But his nose was the most noticeable. It would provide shelter for a family of four in a rain storm.

I said, "Looking for a job?"

He said, "No. I'm looking for the security office for the Fair. My name is Stern."

"I'll be in charge of security for the Fair when it opens. What can I do for you, Mr. Stern?"

Stern said, "Last week, my mother had a visit from someone who said he was with the security for the Fair. He said my father had an accident and was killed. He gave my mother a big chunk of cash, said he was sorry, and left. He didn't tell her what happened to the body. Now, I just discovered that my father was cremated the next day, without any of the family knowing about it."

I said, "All this is news to me. I'm in charge of security for the Fair, when it opens, but the general contractor has that responsibility for now. Maybe it was someone from the general contractor's office. Do you know the name of the person who contacted your mother?"

"She doesn't remember the name, but she said it was Irish because it started with an O."

Blathers asked, "Sure now, and how did you find out your father had been cremated, my good man?"

"I spoke to the people at the morgue. I was away, and only got back in town yesterday. My mother was alone. She doesn't speak good English, and she doesn't have a phone. She didn't know what to do. She just sat and cried until I got home. I need some answers. Cremation is not something we would have chosen for our father."

I said, "Mr. Stern, what you are saying is all news to me. Please give me a day or two to look into what has happened. Is there some way I can reach you?"

Mr. Stern said, "I'll contact you on Friday. If I don't get some satisfactory answers then, I will go to the newspapers." He marched his skinny butt out the door.

Blathers said, "Sure now, we know the victim was a Jew. The way things are in the world today, that in itself may be a motive."

I said, "I'm going to call Mr. Whalen and tell him about Stern. See what he says."

I phoned Whalen. He said to keep our nose out of it if we wanted to keep our jobs.

I said, "Okay. I'll tell that to Blathers."

"Never mind telling anything to Blathers. You'll keep your jobs, but for the love of God, please don't bother with this thing. We want it to go away. I'll deal with Stern."

Chapter 7

We had lunch at the burger joint downstairs and then went upstairs to the office. I said, "You know, what I would like to do is make a list of the things we know. We may know more than we think we do. And as we discover more, we can add it to the list."

Blathers said, "Gee whiz, I thought Whalen said to leave it alone."

"I thought you said not to worry about Whalen."

"I did. Sure, start your bloody list."

I had an easel with a large pad of paper on it. I flipped over the first sheet and on the top of the second sheet wrote "A Stern Problem." Blathers rolled his eyes. Under the heading I wrote:

1. Mr. Stern (don't know his first name) was a Jew.

Blathers said, "Do you mean that as a good thing or as a bad thing about him?"

"Neither. It's only a fact. This list will have only facts, and in the end it should have all the facts that we'll need."

Blathers said, "Fact number two: Old man Stern, whatever his first name is, is dead. And fact number three, he was not killed by accident. Sure, the poor bastard was beaten to death."

As Blathers said "death" there was a quiet knock on the door. I pulled the first page of the pad, the blank page, down to cover our work.

"Come in, please. It's open."

The black dress looked sensational on her perfect figure. She had big dark eyes in a slender face, surrounded by sleek black hair that fell over her shoulders. A pert black hat, with a veil pulled back, was slanted to the front of her head and completed the look. I could only hope. "Are you looking for a job, miss?" Then it dawned on me. She was dressed in mourning.

"No, my father was Jacob Stern. I understand my brother was here to see you earlier today." Now we knew the dead guy's first name.

"Yes, he was, Miss Stern."

"I'm married. It's Mrs. Rhonda Rosen."

I said, "Too bad."

"Pardon me?"

"Oh. I just meant I'm sorry that I assumed you were single."

I like women, and I really liked this one, but I haven't had much luck in that department. I don't have any idea how that little slip popped out of my mouth, and I was somewhat ashamed of my behavior. Anyway, I invited our guest, "Please take a seat, Mrs. Rosen."

She put her pocketbook on the corner of my desk and said she came to see us so we wouldn't take her brother's threat to go to the press too seriously and also because she has been unable to get any satisfactory information from the authorities. It sounded to her, from her brother's comments, that we intended to look into the matter.

I said, "The fact is, our boss told us to keep our noses out of it. He told us it was an accident, and that the family had been compensated." That last part I surmised from the brother's remarks in the morning. A look of discouragement, or maybe surprise, came to her face. I went on, "But between you and us, we have already decided to do some investigating. If you and the rest of your family can be patient, we will see what we can find out."

"Oh, thank you." She extended a gloved hand toward me.

I took it in both my hands. "Why don't you check back with us next week. In the meantime, if you become aware of any other developments, let us know."

She left the office. Blathers had sat there speechless for the whole time, with his mouth open. He wasn't staring at the ceiling and stroking his chin, but I was sure he was thinking, and I knew what he was thinking.

I asked, "And what would your sainted mother say about her?"

Chapter 8

I flipped the blank sheet on the pad over the back, grabbed the next sheet, and tore it off. "See how we learn things. Because we only have the one entry, and now, since we know Stern's first name, we can start again."

Blathers said, "Gee whiz, wouldn't it be just as good if you crossed out the comment about the name and wrote Jacob under it?"

"I like my lists to be as neat as possible." I tore off the part with writing, ripped it into pieces, and put it in the wastecan. I folded the remaining section and shoved it in my desk drawer. "This will make good note paper when I tear it to the proper size. Now let's start again."

On the new second page I wrote:

1. Jacob Stern was a Jew.

2. Jacob Stern is dead.

3. The poor man was beaten to death.

I thought for a moment and said, "I think number four should indicate that we were told by Whalen to keep out of things."

Blathers said, "Sure now, don't you think it would be better if there was no written record of that? If need be, we can always say later that we misunderstood him, unless it's written down somewhere."

"I guess you're right. But it is a very important fact, and we need to keep it always in mind."

"Right you are. I won't bloody forget it."

I asked, "Well, what else should we put on the list?"

"What about the children? Say that young Stern— we don't know his first name—is a funny little fellow. And say that the daughter, Mrs. Rhonda Rosen, is something quite special to look at."

I added:

1. Mr. Stern's son, first name TBD, is a slight man with an unkempt appearance.

2. Mr. Stern's daughter, Mrs. Rhonda Rosen, is a very attractive and intelligent lady.

Blathers said, "Now, you're writing this like you expect someone other than you and me to be seeing it."

I smiled. "You're the one who said not to write something down that you wouldn't want someone else to see."

"Right you are. Sorry."

"I'll keep the blank page over the list, but you never know."

He nodded.

I said, "Now, if there isn't anything more to add, I think we should go up the street to the police station and see what we can find out. Remember, we aren't inquiring about the accident. Let's just say that the fact it happened might be the result of a security lapse, and we don't want any lapses after the Fair opens."

Blathers said, "Ah, lovely. That should keep us out of trouble for a while anyway. Sure, I'll let you do all the talking."

Chapter 9

The Flushing police station was up the street just past the intersection where Kissena Boulevard and 41st Avenue meet Main Street. Desk Sergeant Boyle was on duty. "Goo'day, gents. What can I do for you?"

"Hello, Boyle. Is the captain in?" Mike Boyle knew me. The first thing I did when I opened my office was to call on the local folks. I knew that, in some cases, I would need their cooperation or assistance.

"Mike, this is my new assistant, Blathers. You should become great friends. You both have much the same brogue."

"Pleased ta meet ya, Blathers. How long have ya been away from home?"

"Sure, I've been here two years now. But don't I still miss the old sod."

Boyle nodded his head. "And don't I agree with you. I meself am planning a trip back in August. Me da isn't all that well, and to tell you the truth, it might be me last chance to see him."

Blathers said, "We'll say a prayer for him and also pray that you have a safe journey."

"Thank you, lad. Now, have a seat there, the two of you, and I'll tell the man you're here."

Boyle disappeared into the rear of the station. Then, in a matter of seconds, he yelled out, "Walk this way, gents."

Captain Fitzgerald signaled that we should sit, and said, "What's up?" Fitzgerald was an efficient leader of the local cops. It was his responsibility to keep Flushing a quiet community, no matter what was going on at the adjacent fairgrounds.

"I would like to introduce my assistant, Blathers. He has been here from Ireland for about two years now. His folks were private eyes there, so he was raised in the business."

"Private eye is it? Well, regular policing is a bit different."

I said, "Oh, he's been trained at the police academy here, as well."

"Dropped out, did you, lad?"

Blather answered, "No, sir, I finished me training but didn't join the force, for personal reasons."

"I see, well, that's okay, boy. Now tell me where you're from."

"Drumkeeran, in County Leitrim."

"Ah, the west of Ireland. Rough country."

"Sure, things were getting rough when I left, yes, sir."

Fitzgerald gave Blathers a nod. "Leaving the Old Country behind can be a good way to avoid some rough things, but all too often personal problems can follow you here."

Blathers said, "Right you are. Me sainted mother always said you can't hide from trouble."

I said, "Captain Fitz, we have another matter we wish to discuss with you, a matter of a body on the fairgrounds."

"As far as I know, that whole file has been closed."

"I understand the same thing, but when security

becomes my responsibility, I don't want a repeat incident. Why was Mr. Stern on the property in the first place?"

"You know that his name was Stern? How did you find that out?"

My first mistake. I had to think quick. "I don't recall. I think one of your men mentioned it, but I don't know which one."

"Was it that blabbermouth Boyle?"

"Oh, no, I'm certain it wasn't Boyle." I didn't want to burn that bridge.

The captain looked at me like I was a bad boy in the principal's office. "What else do you know?"

"All we know is there was a body. We were the ones that found it. And somewhere, I don't remember where, I heard the guy's name was Stern. We'd like to find out a bit more so we can take whatever steps we need to, to make sure there's no body found on the grounds while the Fair is in operation."

"Okay, okay, why don't you ask me some questions, and I'll answer them if I can."

"Okay, first, Stern sounds like a Jewish name. Was he a Jew?" Start easy and build.

"I believe he was, yes."

"You know there are a lot of people who believe that Nazi stuff about Jews. Do you think he was killed because he was a Jew?"

"Wait a minute. He wasn't killed. He had an accident."

I said, "Captain Fitz, remember that Blathers and I found the body. We looked it over quite thoroughly before we reported it."

Fitzgerald said, "Get out of here, the two of you,

right now."

So much for an easy start.

Chapter 10

It was raining again, a cold November rain, and a cold wind, as we headed back down Main Street. Depending on what Fitzgerald did now, it could be raining a lot harder when we got to the office. When I opened the door, I knew it was pouring. The phone was ringing like a fire alarm. "Hello. Duff speaking."

"Hold for Mr. Whalen."

"Where the hell have you been? Don't you have someone to answer the phone when you're out? You and your pal Blathers get your asses up here as fast as the IRT will carry you." Slam.

I said to Blathers, "There are some subway tokens in the middle drawer of that desk. Grab a handful and come with me."

It's about a fifteen-minute ride to Grand Central on the express train. Because of the time of day, there were no express trains; they only run during rush hours. We got a local. It takes about ten minutes more. Also because of the time of day, and because Flushing is the last stop on the line, first stop if you're going to the City, Blathers and I got seats next to each other.

As the train ran out of the short tunnel from the underground station in Flushing to the elevated tracks that spanned the Borough of Queens, Blathers asked, "What is your strategy now?"

"I guess we'll tell the truth."

The only sound for the rest of the trip was the clack of the wheels on the track.

****

The main office of the Fair was in the Empire State Building. On the inside of large glass doors, the traditionally luscious receptionist welcomed us. We were expected. "Blathers and Duff, you're to go right in."

I knocked. Whalen yelled, "The two of you get in here on the double."

We placed our hats on a rack and pushed open the door to the big man's private room. Whalen sat looking out the window with his back to us. "Sit and listen to me." We each parked in a chair in front of the huge desk. He swiveled around, and we could see he wasn't quite happy. "I had a call from Fitzgerald in Flushing."

Blathers said, "And faith, didn't we figure that out already."

"Never mind the smart remarks. I told you both to keep out of this thing, and now I find out you know more than you should, and apparently you are trying to find out more than you know. Did you not understand me?"

Blathers wouldn't stop. "Mr. Whalen, we know when we have seen a murder. Is there any reason why a murder should not be properly investigated?"

Whalen shook his head, shrugged his shoulders, and said, "Look, you both know what the world is like today. The Nazis in Germany and their sympathizers here are blaming the Jews for all the troubles in the world. If we push this thing, they will say we are all Jew-lovers, and they'll make trouble at the Fair. On the other hand, if it becomes known that we didn't investigate a murder thoroughly, the Jewish population will be on our case. It puts us between a rock and a hard place. We have already had some of FDR's people in here telling us to keep politics out of the Fair."

Blathers kept at it. "Sure, suppose this murder had nothing to do with politics. Suppose there is a serial killer on the loose. Suppose the body was planted at the Fair site for a reason. Just ignoring this could lead to additional and bigger trouble. Sure, you don't want that, now, do you?"

I said, "And, unfortunately, we have already had inquiries from Stern's family about the circumstances surrounding his accident."

"Damn it! I sent O'Hara down to see the widow. We gave her five grand, figuring that would keep her quiet. Who contacted you?"

I told Whalen about our visits from Stern's son and daughter. He sat back in his chair, looking like he didn't understand what was happening.

Blathers spoke up again. "As me sainted mother would say, something smells a bit fishy here. Don't you think so, Mr. Whalen? Perhaps if you trusted us a bit with some more information, we could help you figure it out."

"No, no. I want you to stay out of it. I'll take care of it. Go on back to Flushing, now, and don't meddle in this anymore."

As we left the office, we could hear Whalen say, over his intercom, "Get me O'Hara, right away."

****

When we got to the lobby, Blathers said, "Did you hear him call for his man O'Hara?"

"I did."

27

"Well, it's late in the day, now, and sure, there's a nice little pub across the street there. I suggest that we get a glass of beer and watch to see if anything happens."

I said, "Don't you remember? I don't drink beer or other types of alcohol. All I drink is water and tea."

Blathers looked at me out of the corner of his eye, shook his head, and said, "Oh, right, well, come along anyway. I'll buy you a nice cup o' tea."

"They serve tea in pubs?"

"Why, certainly. Many of the ladies prefer tea to beer and liquor."

I went into the place with Blathers, and he steered me to a high table in the window, where we could see the front of the Empire State Building. A young Irish fellow asked what we wanted. "I'll have a glass of Piels and a pot of tea for me friend." Our beverages arrived, and Blathers gave the young fellow fifteen cents. I believe there was a generous tip of a nickel in the payment. I am told that a good waiter can often make much more than the twenty-five-cent minimum wage recently mandated by federal law.

Blathers was nearing the end of his beer, and I was enjoying my tea. It was much nicer than I expected it would be. Then we saw a fellow emerge from the Empire State Building entrance. Blathers said, "I bet that's him. That's O'Hara. I feel for sure he's Whalen's boy. Look at that swagger. Let's follow him. I didn't get a good look at him, but with that walk, he'll be easy to follow." He swallowed the rest of his beer and was out the door before I could move. When I got to the street, I saw him going into the 7th Avenue subway station. That was the last I saw Blathers that day.

Chapter 11

When Blathers arrived in Flushing the next morning, he had a donut and paper cup of coffee in hand. Before I could ask, he told me of his adventure. "The fellow got off the train at 14th Street. Sure, I followed him east a few blocks and south a few blocks, and didn't he finally go into a four-story walkup. I waited outside for a while, and then didn't I see our friend young Stern go into the same building. About ten minutes later, O'Hara came out of the building and headed for the subway. And sure, wasn't I just about to go and look at the mailboxes when—oh, gee whiz— didn't the very lovely Mrs. Rosen come out. So I tailed her but lost her at the corner when she grabbed a cab. There was no chance to catch her, so I got on a bus over to 1st Avenue. Murphy's is on 1st, don't you know."

I said, "What's Murphy's?"

"Isn't it just the best pub in Manhattan. They have six dart boards, and Harp's on tap. It's a bit like home."

I said, "It sounds like fun. Anyway, it seems that things smell even more fishy than they did yesterday. We should investigate a little more and hope Whalen doesn't catch us. I have someone coming in for an interview in a few minutes, but after that, perhaps we could spend a few more subway tokens on a trip in to Manhattan."

The person for the interview arrived, and I spoke to

her about being a secretary for the office. Whalen had chastised me for not having someone to answer the phone while I was out, so when I got back to the office the day before, after Blathers had run off, I called an employment agency. The lady said they would have someone at my office at nine the next morning. The somebody was perfect, not sexy, like Whalen's girl, but neat and, at least I thought, smarter than most office girls. After she accepted my offer and agreed to start right away, I introduced her to Blathers. He had gone out for more coffee to allow a bit of privacy for the interview. As he entered the door, Miss Shay—her name was Maggie Shay—asked if she could help him. "But I work here," he said.

I stepped in. "Blathers, this is Miss Shay. She will be doing our clerical work and watching the office when we're away."

Blathers said, "Gee whiz, how do you do, Miss Shay."

"Good morning, Mr. Blathers. It is very nice to meet you. I hope you will enjoy having me in the office."

"And faith, won't I be happy to have someone as nice as you to talk to."

I said, "Blathers, you're going to be so busy you will be talking to yourself, and liking it. Grab some of those subway tokens. I think it's time we visited the Stern household ourselves. Maggie, you're in charge. We'll see you later, probably around two."

****

Thursday November 17, 1938
Dear Diary,
I started my new job today. I think I'm going to like

it. The boss is Mr. Duff, who is the Director of Security for the upcoming World's Fair. His assistant is Mr. Blathers. Funny thing, neither of them seems to have a first name. Mr. Duff said just to call him Duff and Mr. Blathers said to just call him Blathers. I told them to just call me Maggie.

It's a temporary job because The Fair will only run for two seasons, and it will shut down in October after the first season, and the second season won't open until the following May. Duff says there will probably be some days that I don't work during the winter layoff, but the office will still be open, on a reduced schedule for that time. I don't mind, because I'm interested in the kind of work Blathers and Duff do. Duff is on temporary assignment from his family detective agency in Chicago, and Blathers is a former NYC cop. Even though I have to answer the phone, do the typing, and keep the files, I'm sure that eventually I'll get involved with the security work. It's a swell opportunity.

Chapter 12

We found our way to the four-story walkup where O'Hara and young Stern went in and Mrs. Rosen came out. We thought it must be the place where the Stern family lives. The weather wasn't bad. The cold rain had stopped, and while it was a crisp day, the bright sun, that is the part of it that was able to sneak between the tenements, had brought the kids out to play in the street. Two raggedy urchins were on the sidewalk in front of the stoop of the building. They had an old tennis ball, and one would throw it as hard as he could against the steps. The other guy was the fielder. If he caught the ball it was an out. If it got past him it was a single, double, or triple depending on how far it went. I think the ball was too worn out for there to be a homer. I didn't ask the score, but I did ask, "Hey, do you kids live in this building?"

"Ain't none o' your business, mister. In this neighborhood we can play wherever we want."

"I just wanted to know if the Sterns live here."

"I don't know no Sterns,"

The other kid piped up. "Yeah, Hermon, the Sterns was them people what rented the fourth floor rear. Remember that guy what came a couple o' times to see them? They did live here, mister, but they moved out last night. I don't know where they moved to."

I asked the kid, "What's your name?"

"Me, I'm Jacob. My mother calls me that, but you can call me Jake."

"Tell me, Jake, how many people were in the Stern family?"

"There were just da three of them—an old lady, the skinny guy, and a neat broad, er, I mean lady."

"How long did they live here?"

"Oh, just a few weeks. They was funny people. I mean they said they was Jewish, but they didn't hang out wit any of da ladies in da building, or go to da Temple, or anything other Jews do. And sometimes they looked one way and sometimes they looked different. You know what I mean? Like they was going out trick-or-treating or something. Like sometimes the old lady was very old, and then other times she wasn't so old. And sometimes the good-looking lady had black hair and sometimes she was a blonde."

I said, "Thanks for the info, boys. Here's a nickel for each of you, for being such smart boys."

Jake said, "Gee, thanks, mister, but Hermon didn't tell you nothing. Shouldn't I get his nickel too?"

Blathers laughed and said, "Sure, now, look, you two are best friends, are you not? Now, best friends share and share alike, they do. If Mr. Duff gave both of the nickels to you, Jake, you would certainly want to give one to your best friend anyway, wouldn't you? So he just saved you the need to share."

Both boys smiled at each other and shoved their nickels deep into their pockets, wondering aloud how best to spend their newfound wealth.

Chapter 13

Back in Flushing, Blathers and I sat like two little boys, not quite as tough as Jake and Hermon, with our hands in our pockets, wondering what to do next. We weren't at it long when the phone rang. "World's Fair Security. This is Miss Shay speaking. Yes, Mr. Duff is here. Oh, I just started today. Who should I say is calling? Mr. Whalen?" I nodded and Miss Shay said, "Please hold for Mr. Duff, Mr. Whalen."

"Hello, Mr. Whalen. What can I do for you?"

"Have you been messing in this Stern business again?"

"I haven't been messing. Blathers and I went to call on the family this morning. We had promised the daughter, Mrs. Rosen, that we would let her know if we had found out anything further about her father's, ah, accident. When we got there, the family had moved."

"How did you know where they lived, and that they had moved?"

Nailed again. "Why, the, the son mentioned where they lived when he was here last week. We weren't quite sure which building it was, but there were some kids playing in the street. They knew the family and told us they had moved." I chuckled. "Those darn kids know everything that happens in their neighborhood." One more little chortle. "What they don't see for themselves, they hear their mothers talking about on the front stoop. You know what they say, little pitchers have big ears."

Whalen yelled loud enough that Blathers heard him across the room. "Never mind the bullshit. Dig your hands into your stash of subway tokens, and the two of you get your asses up here at three o'clock. The FBI wants to talk to you." Slam!

****

Once again, the very sexy secretary knew us as we walked in. "Blathers and Duff. Go right in, but…" she whispered, "be very careful. Them two Feds have been there for more den an hour grilling da boss." Very softly and very slowly she said, "He ain't going ta be in no good mood." I couldn't help wondering how she answered the phone.

Blathers said, "So it isn't just us the FBI wants to talk to. Am I not surprised? Let's go, Duff."

Whalen was sitting behind his fortress of a desk, but it wasn't providing him much protection. One guy was stretched out in a chair right in front of him, so close he could drool on the mahogany top. His hat sat on Whalen's desk. We wouldn't dare to even bring our hats into the office.

The other guy was pacing from side to side in the room. His hat was also on the desk, beside that of his partner. I can just imagine what would have happened if Blathers and I had come in here and put our hats on the boss's desk.

Whalen stood up as we came in. "Ah, at last, here are Mr. Duff and Mr. Blathers. I'm sure they will be able to provide you gentlemen with some of the information you need. Blathers, Duff, these are agents Brown and Kowalski from the FBI. Use my office for your conversation, gentlemen. I'll run downstairs and get a haircut."

Kowalski, the one who had been pacing, said, "We want you to stay, Whalen. Just sit there and listen."

The few hairs Mr. Whalen had on his head seemed to stand straight up. They really didn't need cutting. His face turned a deep crimson. He rolled his eyes and slumped back in his chair. He finally looked at us, standing there. There was one more office chair available, but no one was sure when Kowalski would sit down. Blathers and I remained standing. Mr. Whalen snapped on his intercom. "Belinda, bring in two folding chairs, please." Then he turned to Kowalski and said, "But I'm not responsible for what happened. These two were the ones who started it all."

Brown wiggled in his seat, shrugged his shoulders, and said, "Mr. Whalen, it appears to us that if these two men had been allowed to investigate the situation, you would not be suffering the embarrassment of having been scammed."

Blathers said, "Scammed? Faith, now, who was scammed? What was the scam?"

Brown began to explain. "The people that you knew as the Sterns were in fact a family of grifters named Ullman, we think. At least we know that the head of the gang is a woman who sometimes uses the last name Ullman. They used to be in the theater, but since that hasn't been as lucrative as it once was, they have turned to the con game. They are now $25,000 richer than they were last week."

Blathers said, "$25,000? I thought you said you gave them $5,000."

Brown said, "He had his man give them another

$20,000 yesterday."

Whalen started to stutter. "B-b-b-but—"

Brown said, "No buts about it. They hit you for $25,000. That's more than most people make in fifteen years."

Blathers said, "Sure, all right, there was a scam, but there was a murder. If them folks weren't who they said they were, who was the murdered guy?"

Brown said, "Probably some Bowery bum that they found already dead from drinking and exposure. They probably just beat up the body to make it look like he had been beaten to death. We don't believe the Ullmans are murderers. Of course, since the body was cremated before an autopsy could be done, we will never know." He glared at Whalen. "The evidence has been destroyed, destroyed by a public official."

I said, "Mr. Whalen had the body cremated?"

Whalen answered, "I didn't know what else to do with it."

One of the FBI men said, "You know that you violated a law, don't you?" Whalen sank into his chair and shook his head. The FBI guy shrugged like he wasn't interested in pursuing the matter, because they started to ask us a few questions about the Sterns or Ullmans. We suggested that they go and talk to the neighborhood kids where the Sterns had lived. Blathers said, "Sure, won't you be surprised how much information you can get for a few nickels."

They seemed satisfied that neither Whalen nor Blathers and I were really guilty of anything except stupidity. Kowalski said, "If you run across these characters again, call us." He handed Blathers and me each a card with his contact information. Whalen extended his hand for one, but the two feds were out the door before he got one.

Blathers and I got up to leave. I said, "We'll be going back to Flushing now, Mr. Whalen. If it's okay with you?"

Blathers said, "I'll be phoning me father in Ireland this evening, Mr. Whalen. I'll tell him how much I enjoy being on your staff for the Fair. He'll be glad to hear of our adventures. Good day, now."

****

Friday November 18, 1938

Dear Diary,

One interesting thing happened today. A Mr. Whalen, who I guess is the big boss of the Fair, phoned. He sounded as mad as a wet hen and asked for Duff. Duff took the call, and as soon as he hung up he grabbed some subway tokens and said he and Blathers would be with Mr. Whalen for some time. I wonder…if they will get fired, and this job will be more temporary that I thought.

****

Monday January 16, 1939

Dear Diary

I've been working for the Fair for about nine weeks now. It has been interesting, particularly since my bosses, shall I say, are a strange duo. Almost like Mutt and Jeff.

Duff is tall and thin, a very well-organized man. As I understand it, when he first gets up each morning, he makes a list of all he has to do that day. And, my gosh, you can set your watch by his arrival at work. Every day at exactly five minutes to nine the door opens and in he comes. I have also heard that once a week on

Thursday night, after he leaves control of security in Blathers' hands, he goes home, puts on his best bib and tucker, takes the Long Island RR to New York, has dinner at a little French restaurant, and goes to the opera, or a play. He only drinks tea.

Now Blathers, on the other hand, is somewhat shorter and a little on the chunky side. He's a seat-of-the-pants guy. He usually works the late shift, but he may show up any time between 10 a.m. and 3 p.m. When he gets there, he'll look around and then decide what needs doing. They tell me that, quite often, on his way home at night, he will stop at a beer joint near his place in Manhattan, where he'll drink a pint or two, chat up the ladies, and shoot darts until closing. I guess that after those nights, the following days are the days he comes in at three.

While I respect Duff for his controlled lifestyle, I'm really interested in Blathers. It is a swell job.

Book Two: "I am a Jew."
Chapter 14

The World's Fair opened on Saturday April 30, 1939. Franklin D. Roosevelt gave a speech. Mayor LaGuardia gave a speech. Albert Einstein gave a speech. Thousands flocked to see "The World of Tomorrow." Duff assumed responsibility for security. I was his right-hand man, and we hired most of the folks who were working for the contractor. We also added a couple of folks who came by for interviews. Most of the contractor's men looked like security guards. Duff and I agreed we needed a few folks who could operate under cover, so to speak.

I had proposed a plan for the opening. "Sure, it seems to me that the pickpockets will be our big problem on opening day. I think if we make it too dangerous for pickpockets to pick pockets, they'll go elsewhere to pick pockets, won't they. If we round up a bunch of them in the first few hours, the word will get out, and the ones we haven't caught will scram."

Duff asked, "What do you have in mind?"

"Well, now, let me take a dozen of our folks, women and men, and dress them up as yokels. They'll look like easy marks, won't they, but they'll be easy marks with handcuffs. We'll have each covered by a uniformed man, and as soon as the pickpocket strikes, he gets arrested. We'll throw them all in the hoosegow and hold them overnight, all in one cell. They won't come back again."

"Sounds like a great idea."

On opening day, we had all of our people arranged in groups with specific duties. Some were assigned to the entrances and exits, to make sure all was calm at those locations. Others were on patrol in various areas. The fair was divided into zones. For example, there was a Food Zone where companies who packaged and sold food were located. There was a Transportation Zone. The auto manufacturers and airline industry showed off their ideas for the future. I thought I might like a car, but I couldn't imagine flying in an airplane.

There was a Communications Zone where television was introduced. FDR's speech was actually broadcast to various places in New York City over TV. There was a Government Zone where countries of the world had their pavilions. And, of course, the most popular zone was the Amusement Area. One of the features of the Amusement Area was the Bendix Llama Temple, which housed a girly show. The most popular place, though, was the Beer Garden. We assigned an extra contingent of people to the Amusement Area. I selected folks from units in each of these sections to establish my "pickpocket flying squad" as I called it.

It worked: within hours we had fifteen of those pocket-cleaning experts crowded into our first cell. There was standing room only. Duff and I went down to see the results. I addressed the guard. "What's this, then? All these folks in one cell? Take that one woman out of there, and put her in a cell by herself."

The remaining fourteen men began to grumble. Even with the woman gone there was only one seat, and that was the toilet. "How long are you goin' ta keep us here? We can't stand forever. It's beginnin' ta smell bad in here."

I said, "Sure, don't I know it doesn't smell too good. That's why I took the woman out. Now you fellows just make yourselves as comfortable as possible. We need to keep the other cells for some of the really bad guys. You all don't want to be locked up with drunks carrying knives, now, do you?" The grumbling got louder. The prisoners realized they weren't going to get any relief.

Fogarty was in charge of the jail for that shift. He had two assistants with night sticks. The jail was a dozen iron cages linked together with metal clamps, so there was always the chance that if all fourteen prisoners pushed on the walls of the cage at the same time it would come apart. The night sticks would be the only protection the jailers had.

Fogarty said, "Mr. Duff, we searched every one of these rascals before we put them in the cage. There's a whole pile of stuff they must have got before we got them. What should we do with it?"

I said, "See if you can identify the rightful owners, and we'll try to get it back to them. Some of them might be making inquiries at the lost-and-found already. Otherwise, if we can't find out who owns it, we'll turn it over to Mr. Whalen, and he'll do with it what he wants, won't he."

Chapter 15

My plan seemed to work. The next morning, we released fourteen exhausted, smelly men and one enraged woman. She said her privacy had been violated. The cost of making a mistake by hitting on one of our local yokels became common knowledge among the pickpocket community. Picking pockets slowed to a snail's pace.

I told the assembled captives, "We're going to release all of ya now, without further ado. But your experience should be a warning to you all. We had some little trouble finding the keys to the cells this morning, didn't we. It was a good show for you all we made a careful search for the darn things, or you would all be there for another day. 'Tis funny how those keys keep going missing. And, oh, gee whiz, yes, don't forget to tell all your friends about our luxurious accommodations and delicious meals."

One prisoner said, "What about our belongings?"

"And what belongings are you inquiring about, now, me good man?"

"When we came in here, them jailers took all the money and other things we had on us."

"Ah, those belongings. Well, it seems that not all of those belongings belong to the likes of you. They will be returned to the rightful owners."

The prisoner kept up. "I was the rightful owner of

the cash I had on me. I want it back."

Blathers said, "Oh, the cash. Well, we have made a careful inspection of all the cash, haven't we, and none of it had your name on it, so, as far as we can tell, none of it was yours. We did find some bills that we had marked and given to our folks. Are you now saying *that* money is yours? Because if you are, then we'll have to turn you and the marked cash over to police, now won't we. Here's what we will do. We will give each of you a quarter, so you can get a subway token and stop at Nedick's on the other end of the line for breakfast."

The troublesome prisoner persisted. "I had fifteen bucks when I was thrown in this shithole you call a jail, and I want it back."

"An' faith, we'll have to go through the money again, and see if we can identify yours. Won't you kindly step back into the cell while we make our investigation."

I nodded to Fogarty. He stepped forward, placed the end of his nightstick in the prisoner's solar plexus and pushed him back into the cell. The jail keeper slammed the door shut, clicked the lock, looked at me, and said, "Oh, me gosh, boss, did I give them keys to you?"

I said, "No, Fogarty, I gave them back to you,"

"Oh, me gosh, I don't seem to have them."

"Well, we will have to find them. We need to let this fellow out as soon as we find his fifteen bucks. The rest of you are free to go. Now, each of you get a quarter from Fogarty, and don't let us see you here again. There is no key to one of these cages, and haven't I forgot which one it is. If we nab ya again, you'll probably end up sharing with this fella here, or in the cage with no key. Picking pockets at this Fair is risky business."

The next day, the squad picked up two crooks. They threw them in with the persistent prisoner, who asked when he was going to be released. "As soon as we find your fifteen dollars."

"I've given it a second thought. I believe I was mistaken about the fifteen bucks."

I said, "Well, don't worry. We think we may have found it. We'll soon know. In the meantime, we would appreciate it if you would tell these lads how pleasant it is here."

All three prisoners were released the following day. They had been provided with soup so they wouldn't starve, but the cage had not been cleaned, so they didn't have much appetite. "I'm so very sorry," I explained to the complainer, "but we just weren't able to find your money." Each of the men was given a quarter, and they were never seen again.

Chapter 16

The Fair was the Fair. People came from all over the United States, and other countries, to view the wonders of tomorrow.

Some came for learning. Some came for levity. Some came for larceny. Duff and I had our hands full protecting the honest citizens from the dishonest ones. One of the favorite spots for the visitors, as I said before, was the Beer Garden. Each night it was bulging with both honest and dishonest folks. When I worked the late shift, four p.m. until closing, I made it a habit to check in at the Beer Garden frequently. And while I liked beer as well as the next fellow, I took my responsibilities seriously and abstained from any beverages until after closing. It was during one of these visits that I saw her.

****

Sunday May 7, 1939
Dear Diary.
After church today, I stopped and bought a paper and went to The Acropolis for a ham and cheese omelet. The Greek omelet gives me heartburn. Next Sunday is Mother's Day, so I'll travel up to Ithaca to see Mom and Dad. They're both from the old country, but they have been here since they were children. They are retired now. They both had good jobs at a big university there, in the food services area. Mom used to

say that those boys put away a ton of food. I was just thinking that when my food arrived.

I was through with the funnies and looking for the crossword puzzle when I noticed a news story about Jewish immigrants. I had heard Blathers talking to Duff about how Jews were being treated in Germany, so I was interested.

It seems there is a boatload of Jewish immigrants who have been trying to escape to Cuba. Apparently it has become a common place for them to go. Then the other day, some guy made a speech to the Cuban Congress. He said he was against this Jewish invasion. He said Cuba must react. If they didn't, Cuba would be absorbed, and the day would come when the blood of Cuban martyrs and heroes would have been shed only to enable the Jews to enjoy the country conquered by Cuba's ancestors. Jeez, the guy is Spanish. Is he talking about the Spanish guys who killed off the people that originally lived there? The reporter said he thought the guy was a Cuban Nazi. I guess there are Nazis all over the place.

The thing is, the Cuban Congress then passed a decree prohibiting repeated immigration of Hebrews, who they said have inundated their country. I wonder what will happen to the poor people on the boat.

****

The Monday after I saw her, I met with Duff. "I'm sure it was her, aren't I. I wouldn't easily forget a looker like that. Now, of course, there is a new disguise. Now she's a blonde. Should we call the FBI?"

Duff asked, "What was she doing? Did it seem she was doing something crooked?"

"She was only having a beer with a guy."

"What was he like? Is there any chance it was the brother in another disguise?"

"I don't think so. He was a big fella, taller than I remember that the brother was. He had a bald head and looked anything but Jewish. He had some tattoos, but I couldn't make out what they were."

"Well, just keep an eye out and let me know what you think is going on. As it looks now, our girl was just having a beer at the Fair with a friend. That's what we want people to do."

"What about the FBI?"

'This lady is a blonde. The other woman had black hair. They don't look like the same person. Maybe they aren't the same person. We don't want to set the FBI off on a wild goose chase, now, do we?"

****

I kept an eye on the Beer Garden that night and the next three nights. The blonde was there with a different guy each night. And, although they all looked like the guy from the first night, there was no doubt they were each different men. I say the all looked alike because they were all large men with little or no hair on their heads and they all had tattoos. Since I was observing from the perimeter of the facility, I wasn't able to see just what the tattoos were, but I planned to see them close up.

****

The next night I wore a dark suit, a white shirt, and a striped tie. A fedora cast a shadow on my face. To the best of my recollection, Mrs. Rosen had never seen me in anything but what might be called work clothes.

I bought a beer for myself and one for the young lady who was assisting me in this instance. None of our female operatives who worked the night shift looked like a sweet young thing, so I enlisted the assistance of our secretary, Maggie, to act as my date. We took a table in the same area where our suspect usually sat. We were just another lovely couple enjoying the evening. As I thought that Maggie was very attractive, I was really enjoying the evening.

"Now, Maggie," I said, "we're to look like everyone else, but the real reason we're here is to get a good look at a particular lady and the gent she is sitting with. I'll see some things, and I'm counting on you to see some things too. Sure, together we should come up with a good description of them both. And, gee whiz, if the guy has tattoos, I want you to be sure to take a good look at them. When they show up, I'll rub me chin and look in the opposite direction. You'll know that they're at a table in the direction where I'm not looking. Got it?"

"I do. Mister Blathers."

And didn't she have a lovely Irish lilt in her speech.

Sure, we chatted for a while. Quite pleasant it was. We were just about half through our beers when the woman and a man showed up. I had not seen him before, although he looked much like the previous gents. They sat at a table to my right. I looked to the left, and Maggie gave the new couple a big smile, while she was giving them the onceover.

I adjusted my hat. The damn thing stood so high on my head I felt like a fool. My whole life I wore nothing but a flat cap. But the fedora cast a grand shadow on my face, and I was able to look back to my right and survey the situation. The tattoo on the back of his hand

49

was my focus, and I could see it was a swastika.

****

Friday June 9, 1939
Dear Diary,

I'm home very late, but it has finally happened. I'm in on the action. Tonight, Blathers had me accompany him to the Beer Garden on a stakeout. There was this great-looking woman and a guy that looked like a thug came and sat next to us. Blathers told me to keep my eyes open and remember all I could about the two of them. That was the best part, but not the only part. I really liked being with Blathers, and he seemed to be enjoying himself. I think he is a good egg. I hope he likes me and will ask me to help him some more. Well, that's all for now. I'm beat.

****

When Duff got to the office the next morning, Maggie and I were waiting. He said, "Blathers, I didn't expect to see you so early. And Maggie, I thought you would take the morning off. How did you like being an undercover operative last night?"

Maggie said, "It turned out to be an interesting evening."

I told Duff about the new man with Mrs. Rosen, although that probably wasn't the name she was using now, and for that matter probably wasn't her name at all. I also told him about the swastika tattoo. He just grimaced without comment. "They sat and had a couple of beers together. They chatted, and we could hear some of the conversation. At first it sounded like this was a blind date arranged over the phone."

Maggie said, "Yeah, but then we couldn't hear the talk because they started whispering to each other. And then the woman started to rub his arms. And she put her hands on his chest. And then, she put a hand on his thigh."

I added, "And then they finished their beers and got up and left."

Duff said, "She's acting like a hooker, but if she's a con, why would she be hooking?"

I said, "I think we need to get to the bottom of this. I'll figure a plan, and we can discuss it tomorrow."

Chapter 17

My cousin Bernie is a cab driver in Manhattan. He works the streets during the day, and sometimes in the evening he will take a special fare. When I presented my plan, I talked Duff into letting me hire Bernie for the evening. I don't drive myself, no need to in the city. Someday I might want to learn, if I eventually make some money without the help of Tammany Hall—they're not much help these days anyway. With a few bucks in my pocket, I might move out to Port Washington. I'd get a little white Cape Cod, not too far from shore. Now, wouldn't that be swell.

I spotted her in the Beer Garden again, with a different guy cut from the same cloth as the others, same muscular build, same short haircut, same strut. Then I went out and met Bernie. We waited in a place outside the main gate until they came out, and jumped in a cab that seemed to be waiting for them. "Do you know that cabbie, Bernie?"

"No, I don't. The cab looks a bit odd. Sure, I don't think it's a regular licensed cab. But then, there's no question he was waiting for the two of them. Didn't I see him turn down a couple of fares before they came along."

"Well, now, follow them as close as you can, but don't be letting them catch on to us."

A quarter of an hour later, the cab we were

following pulled into some tourist cabins on Northern Boulevard. We drove on past, gave it a few minutes, and turned back and parked in front of the cabins. The cab we'd tailed was gone.

We waited. We watched. We wondered. Soon a new Hudson Country Club Convertible parked in front of cabin number six. Bernie said, "Wow, isn't that just a lovely car, now."

A guy jumped out of the car and crashed through the door of the little building. The door slammed shut behind him, and we heard loud shouting. I said, "Let's go, Bernie."

Bernie said, "I only drive." So I felt for the gun under my left armpit, jumped from the car, and banged through the door myself.

The scene inside would have been funny if the guy from the Hudson wasn't swinging a six-shooter in the air. He was wearing blue Levis, a fringed shirt, and a cowboy hat. I hadn't noticed the hat when he got out of the car. He must have had it in his hand and slapped it on his head as he pushed open the door. The other guy, the burly guy from the Beer Garden, was dressed only in his undershirt. The shapely Mrs. Rosen was displaying that fabulous body of hers in a pink bra and pink panties. I thought the guy from the Beer Garden must be really scared. I was sure I could hear his knees knocking together.

I heard a Texas drawl: "I'm a-takin' my wife back ta Texas, and I'm a-gonna shoot yar balls off."

The girl said, "No, Bo honey, please don't." Just then the cowboy swung around and got the drop on me. I ducked into a corner of the room and huddled there. The Texan kept coming at me. The door opened behind him, and Bernie smacked him on the head with a Yankees baseball bat.

I let out a sigh and said, "Gee whiz, Bernie, I didn't know you were a Yankees fan."

Bernie said, "You bet. This is the Babe Ruth model, don't ya know."

The muscleman was still a little speechless. But when he saw the cowboy go down from Bernie's homerun swing, he reached for his pants. Apparently he was prepared to leave his knickers behind, if he could get out of there in a hurry.

I took the bat from Burnie and pushed the fat end into the chest of the big brawny brute. He fell back and landed on the bed, with his private parts still exposed. I said, "So what's going on here, now. Sure, if'n you talk now, you might get away easy."

"This woman made a date with me at a bar on the Upper East Side, near 86th Street. We agreed to meet at the Fair. Then she suggested we come here for a little fun. I asked her how much, and she laughed. She said that because I looked like it would be a really good time, if I paid the cab fare, that would be my only cost. She said her brother owned the cabins, so it would be all right. We were just getting to it when the cowboy busted in. Then you busted in. Now, all I want to do is to bust out of here."

Then the girl started in. "Oh dear, oh dear! If I only had enough money for bus fare, I'd take Bo and me back to Texas, and everything would be okay."

Muscleman reached for his pants and pulled out his wallet. "How much do you need?"

"Two hundred would pay for the bus and give us enough cash for some food along the way." Tears were starting to run down her cheeks. "I just want to get us back to Texas."

"I only have a fifty and a ten left."

The girl said, "I'll take it."

I said, "Save your money. Put your clothes on and scram. This is a scam."

He dressed in a flash and ran out the door. Bernie watched him through the front door. "He's started walking toward Manhattan."

I said, "He got off easy."

Chapter 18

The girl tried to grab the bat from me. But, so there was no injury and no misunderstanding, I dropped the bat and pushed her, with one hand on each shoulder, onto the bed.

She said, "You son-of-a-bitch. We need that money."

"Why? Now, didn't you just get twenty-five grand from Whalen? I'd think that should have provided a luxurious trip to Texas for you and hubby Bo. Is he Bo Rosen then, the Yiddish cowboy?"

She sat up on the bed. "You think you're funny, and that we're just grifters, don't you."

"That's what the FBI guys think. They also don't think your name is really Rosen."

"The FBI! That J. Edgar Hoover is one of the biggest Nazis on the face of the earth."

"Is that right? Am I to understand you don't like Germans?"

"Germans are fine. I don't like Nazis, particularly American Nazis like Hoover and Whalen and that dangerous nut, Fritz Kuhn."

It was beginning to dawn on me why all the victims of the scam looked so much alike. They all looked like Nazi soldiers. There were plenty of pictures of them in the tabloids.

I said, "Okay, lady. Now, do you want to tell me

what you've got going on, or should I just call the cops?"

Bernie said, "Blathers, let's just call the cops and get out of here. Doesn't the whole setup look funny, and this guy from Texas is starting to stir."

I picked up the six-gun from the floor and looked it over. "Oh, gee whiz, guess what, Bernie. This gun isn't loaded."

The girl said, "What did you expect? We didn't want to accidently kill somebody."

I said, "Well, me dear, my gun *is* loaded, so why don't you put your dress back on, and we'll do our best to revive the Lone Ranger here. Then you can tell us your story, and then we'll see about the cops."

Bernie said, "I'll wait in the cab." I guess he didn't want to watch the girl get dressed.

I said, "I'll be out shortly. I'm thinking that I don't have anything to fear here."

****

The cowboy had a lump on the back of his head, but he wasn't dead. Certainly, we'd had no idea the gun wasn't loaded. The girl got a towel from the bathroom, soaked it in cold water, and the cowboy pressed it on his lump.

I told the two of them to sit on the bed. "Now, Mrs. Rosen, Is it Mrs. Rosen, or are you using a different name now?"

"My real name is Frieda Ullman. I am not married. I am an actress, but because of the depression, and because I am a Jew, I am not on stage at the moment. I am the head of a small group of actors, mostly Jewish, who are also unemployed. Yes, we are con artists, but we do not consider ourselves criminals."

I said, "Well, me dear, sure there's plenty of folks would consider you criminals, including the cops, and of course not to mention the FBI."

Frieda argued, "We are not criminals because, while we do pay some of our expenses out of the proceeds of our—shall we call it—off-stage acting, most of the money goes to a good cause."

"Oh sure, and what good cause is that, now?"

"Look at it this way. Who are the—I don't want to call them victims; call them marks."

I said, "Okay, let's start with Whalen."

'Yes, let's start with him. His money was our bankroll. We bought the cabins with that cash."

"You own this place?"

"Yes, it is our headquarters now, and some of our members live here when necessary."

"Okay, so why should we consider him as a deserving, um, mark?"

"His politics. He doesn't see Fascism as a threat. He sends money to Irish Fascists like Eoin O'Duffy, sympathetic with Germany and other Fascist leaders. O'Duffy had his Blue Shirts and his Green Shirts and he led the Irish Brigade to fight for the Fascists in the Spanish Civil War. He and his bunch don't realize that if England falls into German hands, the Irish will be next, and they will be seeing Nazi shirts in the streets of Dublin."

Maybe this is a clue to what me da has on the man. I'll bet he knows Whalen is a Nazi sympathizer.

I said, "So this is an anti-Nazi campaign. Why?"

"Because we are mostly Jews. Most of our cash goes to helping Jews get out of Nazi hands. That is our real mission."

She went on. 'I think you already noticed that all the men I met at the Fair were of a certain type. They all hung out in bars on the Upper East Side that cater to members of the Bund. We take their money to save the folks they want to kill. We could have used that cash you cost us tonight to save a family."

I sat and thought about what she was saying. I knew that Irish immigrants hadn't always been treated well. I remembered seeing signs, "Help Wanted. Irish Need Not Apply." Then, there was that story about the refugees on the ship last month, that Cuba and I guess the United States wouldn't accept. According to what I saw in the paper, the U.S. said they had to apply under a quota system. The paper said there were a thousand Jews that would end up in concentration camps. Folks who are being picked on just because of where or how they were born should get some help from somewhere. It was a cinch the U.S. government wouldn't get involved in the situation in Europe. Most folks were saying that America should mind its own business.

I said, "But I thought there was an organization that was already trying to help Jews get out of German hands. Sure, isn't there a committee or something like that, doing the same thing?"

"Yes, the JDC, but that is mostly well-to-do Jews helping other well-to-do Jews. We are poor Jews trying to help poor Jews."

I said, "Okay, then I won't call the cops, and I won't talk to the FBI, but, sure, I can't let you run your little business at the Fair. Find somewhere else for your shenanigans."

****

I got back in Bernie's cab. He said, "Well, what are

you going to do about these people?"

I said, "Oh, gee whiz, Bernie, I've been giving it some thought, now, haven't I. Since the six-shooter wasn't loaded, I don't see there is any crime has been committed. I guess I have made a mistake."

Bernie shrugged. "Well let's get on back to Manhattan. I'll stop at Murphy's, and we can have a pint for our troubles. Since the Fair is paying for the cab, sure, I'll buy the beer."

I agreed, thinking that we had seen the last of—what did she say her real name was?—oh, yes, Frieda Ullman.

Boy, was I wrong.

Chapter 19

It was Thursday the next week when I showed up about three-thirty for my evening shift. Duff was there for the ritual of the changing of the guard. "All's been quiet, Blathers. I guess we've gotten the grifters on the run. They know we are onto them. There is one thing, though. You know those two guys from the FBI..."

"You mean Brown and Kowalski, do you?"

"Yeah, those two. They want to meet with us tomorrow. They said at two. Can you be in a little early?"

"What do they want?"

"They didn't say. Maybe it has something to do with Whalen again."

"I wouldn't be a bit surprised. Whalen is a bit of a four-flusher, in my opinion."

****

The next day I slept late. I had stopped at Murphy's on the way home. Bernie was there. He and Marge, Mrs. Bernie that is, had had a spat. He was drowning his sorrows, even though he seemed quite cheery about the whole thing.

I had a big breakfast about half eleven at a place that serves breakfast all day. Then I caught the IRT out to the Fair. I was there well before the two o'clock appointment. Duff was busy working on the schedule for the next two weeks. We tried to switch people around so that folks weren't working the night shift all the time. Duff was considerate with everyone except me. I was there most nights. It suited me grand. I liked sleeping late. About one thirty I had a hot dog and beer to wash down my breakfast.

Two o'clock rolled around, and the two FBI boys showed up on the dot. They hadn't changed since the last time we met them. Maybe they hadn't even changed their three-piece suits. I hoped they had changed their knickers. There were pleasantries like "good to see you again," and then they got right down to business.

"We are still after that gang that scammed Whalen. We have some information they were running a con out of here. What do you know about it?"

Duff looked at me. I just grinned. "I thought I had seen Mrs. Rosen—I think that was her name—in the Beer Garden one evening. I investigated and discovered I was incorrect. It was another lady that looked somewhat like her, but she had blonde hair, didn't she."

The FBI wasn't satisfied. "Our informant says that you"—they both pointed at me—"were seen at a place in Bayside where there was an attempt to shakedown a citizen."

I said, "And now, who says a thing like that?"

"The citizen who was being victimized."

"I was at some roadside cabins in Bayside with me cousin, Bernie. We were looking for a suitable place for some relatives from the old country to stay while visiting us here in America. Bernie's Marge wouldn't have them at her place, don't ya know."

"Tell us what happened there."

"We went out there one evening to see what was

available. We saw the cabins. I don't even remember the name of the place, or where it was. Bernie drove, don't ya see. We saw a guy going into one of the cabins, and we asked if we could see the inside. He said sure, but there was a problem, wasn't there. When we went in, his sister and her boyfriend were, how should I say it, just getting ready for bed. If you know what I mean. It was embarrassing to me, to Bernie, and to the brother. The sister and her friend didn't seem to mind too much. Oh, gee whiz, she looked delightful in her pink underwear. I guess I have to admit that I didn't immediately turn round and leave, even though Bernie did, being a married man and all."

"Why didn't you call us?"

"Faith, now, why should I call you? I didn't know there was a federal law against getting into bed together."

"Your story doesn't match with what our informant said."

"Well, isn't that a shame. Perhaps your informant is a con man. Have you checked him out, now? Maybe he has a grudge against someone and is just causing trouble. And gee whiz, did you ask just what crime was committed? Was anyone shot? Did he lose any money? Now, what exactly is his complaint?"

Brown said, "Never mind. We think he's being honest with us, and you're just playing dumb. We want to see these cabins. Tell us where they are."

"Now, didn't I just already tell you, I don't remember. For the most part they were rundown or abandoned, not at all suitable for our family." Brown and Kowalski got up and left without another word. They did give both Duff and me the evil eye on the way out.

When we were quite sure the two snoops were not listening at the door, Duff asked, "Why did you make up that story?"

"Why, Duff, now, sure, I didn't make up anything. But if I wasn't quite accurate in my recollection of things, maybe it's just that me memory isn't as good as it should be. In any event, I have me reasons for what I do. By the way, I have an errand to run. I'll be back by four."

Chapter 20

Good luck is good luck. As I went out the front gate, cousin Bernie was dropping off a fare. "Cousin, don't ask any questions now, just take me to those cabins that we recently visited."

Bernie turned on his meter. "Okay, but who's going to pay the fare?"

"I'll owe it to you. Sure, just go quick, now. It's important."

We got to the cabins in ten minutes. I don't know if it was because Bernie drove faster than usual or because the afternoon traffic was light. Bernie waited in the car while I knocked on the door of cabin six. The cowboy, now dressed in a red sports shirt and gray flannel slacks, opened the door. "Where is Miss Ullman?"

"Why do you want to know?"

"Don't waste time. The FBI are on the way."

"She's in the main office, just over there." I turned and ran to the office. She was behind the counter. "The FBI is looking for this place right now. The last Nazi put them on to you." I turned and ran back to the cab. "Let's go. This must be the wrong place. At least it's sure the wrong place for you and me to be seen."

On our way back to Flushing, I filled Bernie in, just in case the FBI questioned him.

Chapter 21

Two days later, J. Edgar Hoover's two puppets showed up at the Fair office again. This time they came unannounced and without an appointment. It was just four o'clock.

Duff said, "You were lucky to find both of us here, since you didn't make an appointment. In the future, please call at least one day ahead."

The boys both got a little red in the face. "We'll come whenever we feel like it."

Duff said, "That's fine as long as you buy a ticket. Now, why are you here?"

Brown said, "We have found the cabins where our informant was victimized."

I said, "You mean the cabins where your informant claims to have been victimized. Sure, did you find out why he was there? Did you find out what his injuries were? Did you find out how much money he had robbed from him? It's a mystery to me why you're investigating a crime that doesn't seem to have happened."

"Never mind!" It seemed that Kowalski could talk. It also seemed he only knew two words.

I went on. "Well, what did you find at the cabins? Sure, was there a notorious gang of thieves, armed with sawed-off shotguns and wearing brass knuckles?"

Brown said, "The location was abandoned, but we

did find a body."

Duff said, "A body?"

"Yes, with a bullet hole right between the eyes."

Duff noticed the concern on my face, and he tried to keep the federal agents focused on him as he asked, "So this is a murder investigation now. Who was shot? Was it another bum from the Bowery?"

Kowalski spoke again. "It was a prominent citizen from the Bronx. He was a jeweler, and he was politically active, trying to get us involved in the European trouble. We at the FBI considered him a loud-mouth Jew." What a speech. Hoover must have sent him back to school since we saw him last. Too bad the school didn't teach him how to respect other people. I didn't think there was much chance Kowalski would work very hard on this case.

Brown said, "We think he was lured to the cabins by the gang. He probably had a lot of cash on him. They robbed him and murdered him."

I was able to recover from the report of the murder. I knew it wasn't a member of Frieda's "association," and I was absolutely sure, because the victim was a Jew, that they had not committed the crime.

I needed to know more. "Faith, what makes you think he had a lot of cash on him?"

Brown answered, "He had been to the bank and withdrew a thousand dollars in cash the morning of the day we found him. He was probably being blackmailed by the gang. After they got the dough, they killed him and ran like the crazy bastards they are."

I thought that it was probably more likely that he intended to make a donation to the cause. I asked, "Did you find out who the owner of the cabins is?"

"We did. They belong to a company named The GJ American Travel Agency. Their address is the cabin's office. There doesn't seem to be any other record of their existence. There are no corporate records or filings of any kind for a company by that name, or any name like it."

Kowalski's turn again. "So here we are again, to kind of urge you to tell us what you know. This is now a murder investigation, and the penalties for aiding and abetting are severe."

Did they send him to law school since he was here last time? I squared my shoulders. "Oh, gee whiz, I don't know anything about any murder."

Chapter 22

By the time I showed up at the Fair the next day, Duff had taken the time to mull things over in his head. He knew I was playing dumb with the FBI, and he was worried. He made me sit down in front of his desk. "Okay, Blathers, what's going on? Level with me."

I knew very well he was entitled to an explanation, but I hesitated to put him in a situation where he would have to lie to the Feds. "You know I haven't been straightforward with Brown and Kowalski. But if I tell you all, you might find yourself in a difficult position with those guys. Sure, you might have to answer some questions you don't want to answer, don't you see. And you don't want to lie to the FBI."

Duff stretched in his chair, the way he does when he has to make a difficult decision. "Blathers, I trust you. If there is a reason for you to keep quiet, then I respect it. But understand, whatever you tell me will be just between us."

Based on recent happenings, there was a murder to be solved. If left to the FBI, they would follow the easy path and the discriminatory path, and Frieda and her associates would get framed for a murder they didn't commit. I decided Duff would be a great help in pinning the crime on the right folks, and it seemed that he was ready, at least, to be coy with Brown and Kowalski, so I told him all.

He said, "So this is a case where the good guys are doing bad things for a good reason, and the real bad guys are running free."

"Exactly. What do you think we should do about it?"

Duff said, "I don't know. Do you have any ideas?"

"Sure, but not any that are worth a damn."

Duff laughed. "I think that since we let these folks get away with conning the boss, we owe it to them to help them duck this obvious frame-up. Do you have any idea who the real killers are?"

"Miss Frieda told me they were getting their marks for the scam they were running at the Beer Garden from certain bars on the Upper East Side. Sure, it must have been one of those guys, who knew about the cabins, that fingered them. If you'll be wanting to stick around here tonight, I'll enjoy one of me favorite sports and go bar-hopping up there."

Duff said, "Sure, go ahead, but keep your mouth shut. You don't sound like anything but Irish."

"Oh, gee whiz, that doesn't matter. The Irish are welcome in any bar."

Chapter 23

The neighborhood on the Upper West Side was known as Yorkville, and was primarily a German neighborhood. It was common knowledge that certain neighborhoods were dangerous for Jews and other people who either weren't white or who came from somewhere else. Some white folks were frightened by people who were different from them. Others just thought they were superior to people who weren't of their racial background. I was hoping that my bragging to Duff about how the Irish were welcome anywhere would work. I was headed for a mostly German area of New York with the expectation that my brogue wouldn't be a problem.

My first stop was called Berghoff Tavern. I ordered a beer. I was careful not to say "pint" because, in this place, beer was served in steins. The plates full of sausage, sauerkraut, and hot potato salad smelled so good, it made me wonder why I liked ham and cabbage so much. I asked the guy standing next to me, "Sure, can a fella get some food served at the bar?"

"No, if you want to eat, go sit at that table over there. The girl will bring you what you want."

"Oh, gee whiz." I stopped. "I mean, I don't like to eat alone. How about you join me, and I'll buy you another stein, and a plate of sausage, if you're hungry."

The guy looked at me, I guess sizing me up. "I just

ate, but I'll take you up on the offer of a drink. After my meal I often have schnapps. Would that be okay?"

"Why, it would be fine. Sure, I'll just be happy for your company. I'm Mike." I made up a name.

"I'm Albert. What is an Irishman doing in this place anyway?"

Time I made up some stuff. "Sure, I was born in Ireland, but me mother was German. Didn't she make the best kraut in the whole world. She and me da ran a pub in the old country, but they often served German food. The place was always packed. She showed the customers there was more than one way to prepare cabbage, don't you know. Besides, that fella over there looks Irish to me." He was a little guy with a tough look on his face, the Jimmy Cagney type.

Albert said, "Maybe he is Irish. He's a big shot, a special friend of Fritz Kuhn." Somehow, he looked familiar to me.

The waitress came over. She was a full-bodied lass, squeezed into a pair of leather lederhosen. I ordered sausage, kraut, and hot potato salad, another beer for myself, and schnapps for Albert. We were becoming great friends. "Do you live around here, Albert?"

"Yah, the whole neighborhood is German. We do our best to keep it that way."

"Does that mean that a good Irishman, part German, you know, can't find a place?"

"We aren't so worried about the Irish. Quite a few Irishmen agree with our ideas. As a matter of fact, Fritz Kuhn, the leader of the Bund, has that Irish fellow you saw earlier on his staff. Like us, many of the Irish want to keep their neighborhoods white and Christian. You know what I mean."

"I do, but what happens if a Jew moves into that building across the street, say?"

"The landlord knows better than to do that. If he does let Jews in, his building won't look so nice, very soon. Plus his rents will probably be paid late. And to top it off, the Jews won't like living there, and that's for sure. We think we should make them live together, if we're going to let them live at all."

I knew I was in the right place to start my investigation.

****

And what happened a few minutes later reinforced my certainty.

"Don't I know you?" A guy approached our table. It was the muscle man from the Bayside Cabins, but he was wearing his pants now. I had to decide quickly how to deal with this. I couldn't pretend he was wrong. I said, "Oh, yeah, I know you, but I didn't recognize you with your pants on."

He said, "Oh no, I made a mistake. You look like someone else." And he was gone.

I said, "Alfred, do you know that guy?"

"I do. He's in a lodge with me and some of the other boys."

"I'll bet your lodge is all German, and a friendly Irishman couldn't join."

Albert looked like he was thinking hard. "He might if he's half German, and also depending on the reason he left Ireland to come to the U.S."

I smiled. "There's lots of reasons to leave an Ireland that's ruled by the British."

Albert smiled back. 'Like maybe a guy was wanted by the authorities."

"Sometimes a man is wanted for things that are done, shall we say, for the sake of freedom, but the authorities don't see it that way and consider it a crime. I hear tell that some folks come to America because of a problem like that."

At this point, it seemed that Albert's little lodge might be looking for a gunman. Or maybe, if they couldn't pin the jeweler's murder on the Jews, they needed a fall guy. A dumb mick would make a perfect foil.

Chapter 24

The next day Duff was waiting on pins and needles to find out what my evening had been like. I gave him the whole story. "Damn, be careful. It sounds like you are letting yourself in for big trouble if they find out who you really are."

"I think they probably already know. The thug from the cabins won't admit that he saw me there, but he will be suspicious, and he will do something to make the others suspicious too."

"I wonder if there's some way we can provide some protection for you."

Maggie had been in and out of the office while we were talking. She could tell there was something up because of my absence the prior evening, Duff's worried look, and our quiet conversation.

She stood in front of Duff's desk with her hands on her hips. "Mr. Duff, Mr. Blathers, I am here. I know there is some kind of caper going on, and I want to help." She pulled up another chair, sat, reached into her purse, pulled out her hand, and plopped a Saturday Night Special on Duff's desk. "Since I helped out in the Beer Garden that night, I've been wanting to do something besides answer the phone. I have been taking pistol training. I'm the only girl in my class. I am taking judo lessons, too. I can throw a man your size flat on his back in just the blink of an eye. And you don't want to know what I could do to your desk if I had a mind to."

****

There she was again in the Beer Garden—Mrs. Rosen, or Miss Ullman. She probably had a different name now, because tonight she was a redhead. She was wearing a canary yellow summer dress. There was a small yellow hat on her head, a string of yellow beads around her neck, and bright yellow casual shoes on her feet. I wanted to talk to her, and it looked like she wanted to talk to me. I couldn't let that happen because, if I approached her, my shadow might arrest her.

Yes, I was being watched. The guy was new, but I knew who he was. Since my last encounter with the representatives of the federal government, several different guys had been on me. They were waiting to see if I would contact anyone in Miss Ullman's group. Even though the evening temperature was eighty degrees, the FBI guy was dressed in a three-piece suit, striped tie, and a snap-brim hat. All my quiet friends had been dressed that same way. It must have been that J. Edgar had a cookie cutter that produced them.

Behind the bar in the Beer Garden there was a phone that connected directly to the security office, to be used in case of trouble. I thought maybe Maggie was still around. She was itching to get involved with our "caper." Luckily, she answered.

"Come up to the Beer Garden and sit down with a lady in yellow. You can't miss her. Tell her that the FBI is near, and it's too dangerous for me to meet with her. Find out what's on her mind and tell her to get out of here as fast as she can."

In just a few minutes, Maggie strolled into the Beer

Garden. She was dressed in blue and looked as good as the redhead in yellow. Maggie spotted Miss Ullman, approached the table, introduced herself, and sat down. She signaled to a waiter to bring her a beer. I suppose she thought that was good cover. Miss Ullman listened, spoke briefly to Maggie, handed her something, got out of her chair, glanced in my direction, and headed for the exit. Maggie finished her beer.

Back in the office, Maggie told me, "She wants you to see a lawyer, Hyman Littlefield. His office is in Great Neck." She handed me his card.

****

I phoned Mr. Littlefield the next morning and made an appointment for one-thirty that afternoon. The problem was getting to Great Neck without my federal companion. The North Shore Line of the Long Island Rail Road served the Fair and ran west to New York. It also ran east to Port Washington. On the eastern trip it stopped at Great Neck.

I reported for duty at the Fair at about noon. The FBI man rode out with me on the IRT from Grand Central Station. He dutifully purchased a ticket. We had sold a lot of tickets to the FBI. They were becoming one of our best customers. He tailed me through the crowd and watched me enter the security office. I didn't want him to know that I knew he was there. I'm sure the Feds thought they were clever by changing the guy tailing me on a regular schedule. They might have fooled me if they had sent someone who wasn't wearing a three-piece suit.

My plan was to walk out the back entrance to the Fair, walk to Flushing, and catch the LIRR to Great Neck at the Flushing station, leaving the FBI to think I was in the security office meeting with Duff. I climbed out the back window of the office, snuck through the area where we had our makeshift jail, climbed over some trash cans, and I was on my way. In half of an hour, I was in Mr. Littlefield's office.

"The reason my clients wanted you to talk to me is that they want to sell the property in Bayside. They want to sell it to you."

I said, "Oh, gee whiz, I would like to help out your clients, but there's two things, you know. Number one is I don't know what I would do with a property in Bayside, and number two is I don't have any money to buy it with."

Mr. Littlefield asked, "Do you know what a motel is?"

"Never heard the word."

"Well, it's a relatively new idea. It's kind of like a cross between cabins, which require a lot of space and a lot of maintenance, and a hotel, but folks can still park their cars in front of their room. The property now has twelve cabins. In the same space we could have a motel with twenty or more rooms."

I said, "Doesn't that sound like a grand idea, but I still don't have any money."

"I have arranged everything. Here's what we will do. My clients sell the property to you, and we arrange a mortgage to pay for it. We already have a friendly bank that will put up the money. We have formed a little corporation to hold the title: Blathers, Inc. It will be quite clear on the record, for all to see, that you own the property. Then you will hire a company to build the motel, and later on, lease it to a company that will run it. It will all look like a regular business deal, but unfortunately you won't make any money. All the income will go for other purposes. The bank will receive its mortgage payment each month. The taxes will be paid. The building will be maintained in tip-top shape, and all the other expenses will be met. Then, one day, when it is safe for my clients to own property, they will buy all the stock in Blathers, Inc."

I said, "Doesn't it sound mighty complicated to me."

Lawyer Littlefield said, "All you have to do is sign a few papers. If you believe in the work my clients are doing, this will be a great contribution to their effort."

Of course, the first thing that went through my mind was that I was dealing with a bunch of con artists. Maybe I was being set up for a big con. Then I realized that if they took me for all I had they would get nothing, so I signed.

Chapter 25

Now I was a grand wealthy property owner, I wanted to get back to what was going on in the Upper East Side. I switched shifts with Duff and was on duty at the Fair first thing in the morning. Maggie asked, "What are you doing here this early?"

"Don't I have some personal business to attend to tonight."

She said, "I'm going with you."

"I don't know why you would want to go anywhere with me."

"You can't fool me. You're headed to that German bar, and I know it. I'll be ready to leave when you are."

"Maggie, me dear, this might be a bit dangerous. You should stay out of it."

"Blathers, me boy, it will be less dangerous if me and the little package I carry in my purse go along. There is no way you can keep me out of this. Either I go with you, or I'll just go and sit at the bar myself. If you don't want to say I am your girlfriend, you can say I'm your sister or cousin."

"Maggie, me dear, I don't think they allow women to sit at the bar, so there."

"Blathers, me boy, that woman we saw in the Beer Garden was able to pick up men alone in at least one of those bars. I'll bet I can do the same. See you there!"

It was no use. "All right. Be ready at six. Don't

change your clothes. If you're going to be my niece—you're too young to be my cousin—you need to be looking modest. By the way, Bernie is your father."

****

It was just about seven when Maggie and I arrived at the Berghoff Tavern. We took a table not far from the bar. The waitress came over. "What are ya drinking?"

I said, "Maggie, what will you have?"

"I'll have a beer. I presume that's what you're drinking, Blathers."

I cleared my throat. "Maggie, you mustn't call me by my childhood nickname. Even though you're my niece, you should call me Mike."

"All right, Uncle Mike."

I looked at the waitress,

"That will be two beers, me dear."

She looked back at me with a frown. "Ya know this is a German place, don't ya?'

"We do, dear. Even though we seem to be, shall we say, not German, we do love grand German beer, grand German food, and grand German folks. What's good to eat tonight?"

"We have sauerbraten with red cabbage. The cabbage is cut very fine."

"It sounds perfect to me. How does it sound to you, Maggie?"

Maggie said, "Make it two orders, and don't delay in bringing those beers."

The beers arrived almost immediately. As we started to sip them, the muscle man from the cabins, the one who'd had his pants off, the one who wouldn't admit that he was there, the one who skedaddled as quick as he could, approached the table. "I need to ask you something."

I figured that maybe I could make a friend out of this guy instead of an enemy. "Sure, sit down. This is my niece, Maggie, and my name is Mike. What's on your mind?"

"Can I talk in front of your niece?"

"Why, sure, she's older than she looks, and she knows about our, shall we say, earlier meeting, anyway."

Our friend wiped his hand across his forehead. "I need to know what you were doing at those cabins that night."

I had an easy answer for that one. "Why, wasn't I in the process of buying the property. I just closed on it the other day. Sure, you can check the records. I'm thinking of building a motel there. Have ya heard of motels, now?"

"I have, yes. Well, that's okay, then. I guess I should be thanking you for getting me out of a bad fix. One more thing, if we can keep our past meeting just between you and me, I'll appreciate it."

"Oh, gee whiz, you need not worry. I'm not one of those washer women, shooting off her mouth."

The meal arrived, and our friend thanked us for the chat and left us to dig in.

As we ate, the bar became more busy, and I saw that my mate from the last time was enjoying a pint—I mean stein. He waved a greeting from the bar, and I waved back. When we finished our meal, I signaled that he should join us, and he pulled a chair up to the table. "Albert, this is my niece, Maggie. Are you ready for schnapps?"

"Why, sure. Thanks, Mike, good to see you again. I

talked to the fellows about you joining the lodge. They're thinking it over, but I just bet you're in."

"Thanks, Albert. I'm sure I'll be a real good, loyal member."

As Albert lifted his stein to his lips, a hush came over the crowded restaurant. I looked to Albert to have him tell me what was happening. He whispered, "It's Fritz Kuhn." He was accompanied by the Cagney lookalike. Besides in this bar, where had I seen that guy before? Probably nowhere, probably I had just seen too many Cagney movies.

I had read about the Nazi Bund meeting on George Washington's birthday. Kuhn had gathered 20,000 Nazi sympathizers at Madison Square Garden. In front of a group of uniformed men, he spoke to a roaring crowd about the Jewish-controlled press, radio, and cinema. He warned against Jewish-led communism and led a "*sieg heil*" salute to Hitler. Then he waved the American flag and declared George Washington the first American Nazi.

"He's head of the Bund. That's his Irish guy with him." Albert continued to whisper. "He's coming over here."

The Nazi leader approached our table. Albert jumped up and raised his arm. "Sieg Heil!" That was a bit of a surprise.

Kuhn answered the salute, pulled up a chair, and sat down, uninvited, at least by me. He looked at me and said, "So you are an Irish fighter, are you?" He spoke with a heavy German accent.

I said, "I'm part Irish and part German, but I was raised in Ireland, so perhaps I think like an Irishman, but I don't know that I'm a fighter."

Kuhn smiled a sly smile. "So I have a former IRA man right here with me. Allow me to introduce my friend, Mr. O'Hara. He is a former IRA man. Mr. O'Hara and I would like to talk with you. Call me for an appointment." He handed me a card, left the table, and began circulating among the crowd, shaking hands. O'Hara tagged along behind him, kind of like a bodyguard. So Cagney is O'Hara. I didn't recognize the face, but now I recognized the swagger.

Chapter 26

Kuhn's invitation was very interesting. I had left Ireland not because the authorities were after me for being a rebel, but because I was tired of finding my friends being arrested for killing someone, or being shot themselves.

I am not sure if I did it on purpose or accidently, but I clearly left the impression that I might be a killer to the folks around East 85th Street. So this looked like an opportunity to maybe find out who killed the jeweler. I called for an appointment. I guess Kuhn had plans for me, because his secretary said she was expecting my call, and could I come in at eleven the next morning.

****

The next morning, I took the local 3rd Avenue Elevated to the 84th Street station, and walked one block to 85th Street. The Bund office was at 178 East 85th, in the heart of Yorkville. When I entered Kuhn's office, I was greeted warmly by a statuesque blonde. She was very good-looking, but not petite. I thought her name might be Brunhilde.

"Mr. Boyle, it is so nice of you to come in. One minute and Mr. Kuhn will be right with you." A slight accent, but she had obviously been in the U.S. for some time. Just then the door to the inner office opened and Fritz Julius Kuhn came bouncing out. "Boyle, come in, come in."

The desk was on the back wall. A large swastika flag hung on one wall, and a large Stars and Stripes hung on the other. I guess the idea was that Nazi thinking and American thinking were the same thing. I wasn't so sure. I sat in a leather-padded chair in front of the desk. Kuhn sat behind the desk. He was not in uniform as I was told he probably would be. He had an unlit pipe in his left hand. He looked like a picture of a college professor I had seen in the newspaper. There was nothing on the desk except, near his right hand, something that looked like it might be a paperweight was covered with a Turkish towel. He also played with a new, unsharpened pencil in his right hand. "So I understand that you want to join the Bund."

I said, "Well, not quite, now. I was somewhat interested in joining a lodge that a fellow, name of Albert, the guy I was with when I met you the other night, belonged to, wasn't I."

"Ah, ya, I know Albert well. His lodge is part of the Bund. Now, membership is restricted to Christian Germans. I know that you say your mother was German, but you probably prefer an Irish pub to a German restaurant. That is why we haven't okayed your membership yet. Therefore, I have a few questions for you, if you don't mind."

"Oh, not at all, not at all."

"First, you go by the name of Boyle, but your property is registered to a corporation named Blathers, Inc. Where does that come from?"

"Oh, gee whiz, that's what they used to call me in the old country when I was a wee lad. I thought it would be a good name for the development company

I'm starting in Queens."

"Yes, you bought the property from a travel company, did you?'

"I did, but you know, I never met those folks. My lawyer handled it all, don't you see."

The interrogation went on. It became clear that they had done their best to check me out. Finally the elephant in the room was put upon the table. Kuhn asked, "Did you know there was a murder at your property?"

"Sure, I did, you know. But it happened just before I closed the deal. I don't really know anything about it."

Kuhn said, "Do you know who the victim was?"

"I haven't the slightest idea, now do I."

"He was a Jew, a Communist, very dangerous, wanted to take away our democracy, very dangerous. If he had his way, our boys would be over in Europe fighting against one of the smartest leaders in history. Hitler will save the white race from the Jewish plot to take over the world." Kuhn jumped to his feet. "Heil Hitler."

This must be a common occurrence in Yorkville. The scene was either the most sincere expression of zeal I ever heard or the craziest thing I ever heard. My first reaction was crazy. This must be the kind of thing that he says at the Bund meetings. I sure as hell didn't want to get involved in that kind of ranting and raving. On the other hand, the reason I was here was to find out more about the killing in Bayside. So far I hadn't found out a thing.

Kuhn regained his composure and sat back in his chair. "So, well. If you would like to help us in our fight against Jewish oppression and Communism, we will consider you for membership. However, membership may be dangerous. Many of our members are armed. You should be too." He pulled the towel off the object on his desk. It was a pistol. He put the pencil in the barrel of the gun and shoved it toward me. "Here, take this, with my compliments." I picked up the gun. I realized that only my fingerprints were on it now.

****

Duff said, "No question about it. You've been made. They know you're not Mike Boyle. By the way, how did you come up with that name?"

"The desk sergeant in Flushing. I needed to come up with something quick, so I thought, who is the most Irish guy I have seen, and I remembered Boyle from the police station."

Duff laughed. "It's no wonder you didn't fool Kuhn. He probably found dozens of Mike Boyles in the phone book, and probably found out that most of them are cops."

I asked Duff, "What do you think we should do with the gun?"

"Here's what I think. That gun may very well be the one used to shoot the jeweler in Bayside. If not that, it was used in some other crime. Only your fingerprints are on it. They want to frame you."

"I think you're right. But how do we get out of the frame?"

"Let's go see your best friend Mike Boyle and Captain Fitzgerald."

Chapter 27

We hadn't visited the Flushing police since the Fair opened. Our security measures were working well, and we didn't need the local police to resolve any of our incidents. Mike Boyle was on duty when we arrived. "Good morning, gents. It's a pleasure ta see ya. They say you're doing a grand job over at the Fair. I've been there a few times meself, and had a wonderful time."

Duff said, "That's nice, Boyle." He handed the officer a packet of free passes. "Be sure to come again, and bring Mrs. Boyle and any other Boyles you would like to have join you. If these aren't enough, just ask for me or Blathers at the gate. We'll come out and get you in."

"Thank ya kindly, Mr. Duff. Now, what can I do for ya this morning?"

"We would like to see Captain Fitzgerald if he's not too busy."

Fitzgerald apparently heard us, because he poked his head out the door. "Ah, you two. Has there been another murder?"

Duff said, "Funny you should ask. Murder is what we need to talk to you about."

Fitzgerald laughed. "Don't you get involved in anything but murder? How about a nice robbery or assault or something easy. Come on in."

We stashed our hats on the coat tree in the office

and made ourselves comfortable in the captain's chairs. Duff began to explain the reason for our visit. "Do you know about a body that was found a while back shot in the head in an abandoned property in Bayside?"

Fitzgerald nodded. "Yes, I know about it. Max Goldman, a jeweler from the Bronx, I think."

"That's the one. Blathers, here, owns that property. He was negotiating to buy it at the time of the murder. The FBI has been around questioning him about the murder. So my first question is, why is the FBI involved in a local murder case?"

Fitzgerald said, "I don't really know. Our guys are handling the case. The FBI said they just wanted to be kept advised of our progress. They had some other case they thought might be connected."

"Are you personally involved in the case?"

"Not really. It's being handled by the homicide squad, but I know all those guys, and it did happen in my bailiwick, so I'm kept up on the case. They do tell me that unfortunately there hasn't been much progress. I guess the widow has been quite upset because we don't even have a lead in the case."

I said, "What about the folks that owned the property before me? The FBI seemed to think they robbed and killed the guy."

"That's what they think, but they don't really have any evidence. Besides, we don't even know who they are. As I understand it, all we have is a corporation name, but there is no record of a corporation of that name. It was a phony front."

Duff looked at me. I shrugged. "I'll tell him," I said. "Sure, Captain, if you had the gun involved in the killing, would that be a help?"

"We have the bullet. If we had a gun, we could tell if it was the murder weapon."

I took the gun out of my jacket pocket. "Try this one."

The captain looked at it with a frown on his face. "Where did you get that?"

"Didn't someone give it to me, in such a way that only my fingerprints would be on it. Sure, I think they are trying to frame me for the killing."

Fitzgerald picked up his phone. "Hold on a minute. Let me make a call." He gave the operator the number and waited until the connection was made. "Good morning, Joe." A pause. "I'm calling about the Goldman case." A longer pause. "Really, he's sitting right here in my office. Yeah, the gun is on my desk." Another short pause. "Okay. I'll keep them here until you get here." A very short pause. "Yeah, there's two of them, the security guys from the Fair."

Fitzgerald turned to us and smiled. "It seems there was an anonymous phone call from a pay phone this morning. The tip was that you killed Goldman, and that you had the murder weapon in your possession. The homicide guys are on their way to talk to you, so sit tight."

"Am I under arrest, then?"

"Not yet."

****

The homicide detective arrived much faster than one would have expected. Maybe he believed the anonymous tip and was afraid I would make a break for it before he got there. Fitzgerald did the introductions. "This is Detective Joe Higgins from Homicide. The Goldman case is his. Joe, this is Blathers and Duff.

91

Duff runs security at the Fair, and Blathers is his right-hand man. I have to say that, by all appearances, these two are doing a bang-up job. I don't think we have been called once for any problem there."

Higgins looked at me like I was the worst criminal he had ever seen. "Look, I don't care who or what you are. We have a tip that you are a murderer. That you are carrying around the murder weapon, and I now find that the tip is probably true."

I said, "But I brought the gun to Captain Fitzgerald. I told him that I thought it was the murder weapon, and I turned it over to him."

Higgins shook his head. "Look, lad, I'm not that long from the old country myself, but if I had killed somebody, and I thought that someone was going to tip the cops, I might run to the nearest police station and turn in the gun. That way I would look innocent even though I wasn't."

Duff said, "Just a second, Detective. Blathers and I have known about this case for some time. The FBI has been following Blathers and bothering me about it for weeks, even though it's not their case. The two FBI guys, Brown and Kowalski, think the actual murderers are some, shall we say, friends of Blathers. We know that his friends didn't do it. So Blathers has been doing a little investigating of his own. Let us tell what we know, and then you can make a decision about why we are here."

Higgins didn't seem happy. Maybe we had made more progress on solving his case than he had, and he wouldn't like that. So I said, "Sure, now, Detective Higgins, we are as interested in getting this case solved as you are. We don't want me or my friends to be wrongly accused, now, do we. So we are ready to tell you everything and let you use it however you want to close your case."

Fitzgerald said, "That sounds good to me, boys. Tell us all."

I told them all I knew. I told how I went to Yorkville and talked to Fritz Kuhn. I told how the gun came to be in my possession. I told about Frieda and her work. "Oh, gee whiz, our friends are a group of folks engaged in a very humanitarian work on behalf of Jewish people in Europe. Isn't that why we know they didn't kill the jeweler. We think that the jeweler made a bank withdrawal to make a gift to the organization. That being said, some of their other fund-raising tactics may be a bit questionable."

I went on to tell of the Jewish situation in Europe, the attitude of the Bund and its members, and the nature of the questionable tactics. I stressed that the only victims of Frieda's group were people who would otherwise spend the money to persecute Jews, as Nazis or Nazi sympathizers. Since the money was used to save Jews from the Nazis, it looked like a win-win for the Jews. "Captain Fitzgerald and Detective Higgins, sure and you will remember how it was to be persecuted because of your nationality or your religion, both in the old country and here in America."

Two Irish cops gave my plea some thought. Higgins said, "The only problem here, lad, is that Fitzgerald and I are sworn to uphold the law."

I nodded. "I understand that, and sure, I would not ever ask you to do something that you didn't think was honorable. But can you look at it this way, now—you don't know that the Jewish group has ever violated the law, just because I'm only saying some silly things without a lick of proof. And you are more interested in solving the murder than anything, are you not? I think if you test that gun, and it is the murder weapon, you have the lead you need, but you will know I didn't do it, and I think you believe that my friends didn't do it either. Now, doesn't that leave you with the Bund? And I'm thinking that, based on what you know now, you'll never pin it on them. They think I'm their sucker. So I say let them think so. I'll hang around with them and play the dumb Irishman. I'll see what I can do to put the finger on someone."

Higgins got to his feet. "Have a nice day, gents. If ya ever meet this Mike Boyle fella, let me know."

Chapter 28

Duff plopped in his chair behind his desk. I sat in one facing him. It was time to plan where to go from here. The door banged open and Maggie bounced in. "You guys are not having this meeting without me. What happened at the police station?"

Duff nodded. I opened my hands and raised them as if I had no control over the situation. Duff told Maggie all about our meeting with Fitzgerald and Higgins. She said, "Well, what do we do now?"

Duff said, "Maggie, we want you to be a help, but we don't want you to be put in any danger."

"Oh, sure, Blathers can be put in danger and that's all right, but I'm just a girl so I need to be protected. Did you forget about Maggie junior?" She banged her gun on the table. "At least I'm armed. If worse comes to worst, I can shoot the bad guys. All Blathers can do is make faces at them."

I said, "Maggie, sure I have a gun, and I know how to use it."

"Oh, yeah, you show up with a gun in Yorkville, and before you know it you'll get shot. Those lugs up there think I'm just a sweet piece of fluff. They'll never suspect that I can put a hole right between their eyes. You need me to protect you."

She was too much for both Duff and me. We included her in our plan. When all was said and done, it was decided that Maggie and I would return to the Upper East Side that night and pretend that we had not talked to the police, and we had no knowledge of the anonymous phone call. Maggie said, "Good, I'll meet you at the Berghoff tavern at nine." What could either Duff or I do to control our new, enthusiastic, aggressive, reckless assistant? I said, "Okay, I'll see you there."

****

When I got to the Berghoff at a little before nine, she was already there, sitting at a table with Albert. In front of her was an empty plate that, based on the gravy stains, had obviously held an order of sauerbraten. I pulled a chair up to the table, said hello to Albert, and looked at the plate. "Sure, Maggie, you came early and had supper."

"A girl has to eat. Albert was kind enough to sit with me while I dined. One does hate to eat alone."

"If I knew you wanted supper, I would have been happy to join you."

"Well. Bla… Mike, you knew I would eat, but you didn't suggest that we have dinner together when we agreed to meet here. I just assumed that you must have another obligation, maybe with that actress friend of yours."

"I don't have any actress friend like you think. Sure, didn't I have a burger in Flushing before I caught the IRT."

"Well, maybe the next time we agree to meet, you will be more understanding."

"Understanding? What in hell do you mean by that, now?"

"Oh, never mind. I had a delightful time, having

the companionship of Albert."

Women are hard to understand. It's no wonder that I am less understanding. I tried to break down the wall that was just built. "Well, what would you like to drink? I'll get you one."

"Oh, that's not necessary. Albert has just ordered us each a schnapps. Here comes the girl now."

The waitress set the two drinks on the table. Albert said, "Get my pal Mike one, my dear, on my tab."

I ordered a beer and sat back to try to appraise the situation. It couldn't be that Maggie had a date with Albert, or that there was any attraction. I couldn't figure what she was up to. In any event, I wasn't sure I liked it.

My beer came, and we all sat quietly while we drank. Maggie finished her schnapps and said, "Well, I guess I'll be going. A girl needs to eat, and a girl needs her beauty sleep. Albert, will you help me find a cab?"

"Sure will. Come on."

I was left sitting alone. I ordered another beer. "Put it on Albert's tab. I'll settle up with him later."

Albert returned to the table. "I put her in a cab. I know the driver. She'll be fine. Say, when you finish that one, Kuhn would like to meet with you. He'll be here in about fifteen minutes. He said he has a job for you. A kind of initiation task into the Bund, I think."

It didn't seem like fifteen minutes before Fritz Kuhn marched through the room like he was the *Führer* of the USA. Albert said, "Give him a minute or two to get settled. He has something like an office in the back room. I think he uses it for unofficial business. He'll send someone for us."

No sooner said than done. As Albert finished

speaking, a door at the rear of the barroom opened and a hand motioned to us that we should come in. Albert went first.

In the makeshift office there was a long table. Kuhn sat at one end and motioned to Albert that he should sit on the side nearest the door, and then he indicated that I should go around the table and sit against the wall. When we were settled, Kuhn began, "Well, Mr. Mike Boyle, did you have an interesting day?"

"Sure, nothing unusual. My boss had some business with the local cops, so I went along with him to a meeting in Flushing. I guess that was the only thing that was different from any other day."

Kuhn said, "You didn't have a visit from the police?"

"Oh, sure, and quite the other way around, now, wasn't it. I visited the police. Of course, since I was playing second fiddle, they didn't speak to me, and I didn't speak to them. Sure, why do you ask? Was there some kind of report or news about me that I haven't heard?"

Kuhn said, "Oh, no, no. I was just worried that there might be some trouble because we have had a meeting. The police are more than interested in our activity from time to time. They have often badgered folks after they have been to my office. I thought they might have talked to you."

"Isn't it like I said. I went to the meeting, but I didn't talk to them, and they didn't talk to me."

Kuhn said, "Not a problem. Now the reason I wanted to talk to you, I wonder if you would do us a little favor." He reached into a bag sitting on the table and, lo and behold, brought out another gun. This one was a German luger. "We have a bit of a problem, and her name is Goldman. She is the wife of the jeweler Goldman. She is trying to blame our organization for his murder, and the terrible thing about it is she has the ear of the Jew-lover Roosevelt. Her husband was big in politics. We need to silence her quickly, and we want you to do the job. Just go to her house, break in, and shoot her. Leave the gun. It can't be traced, so there will be no hard evidence against us, but there will be a message: Jew bastards leave the Bund alone, or you will die."

I picked up the gun. "I don't know how much you know about killing someone, but it isn't that easy." I wanted to sound like a pro, even though I have never even pointed a gun at anyone. "There's the question of alarm systems. There's the question of an escape route. There's a question of when she will be alone. If I break in and she has someone there, I might be the one to get shot. Then the police will be at your door." I picked up the luger. "Give me a couple of days, and I'll get back to you."

I left the restaurant with the luger stuck in my belt. As I approached the corner of the building, a shadow appeared in the ally that ran along the side of the restaurant.

"Blathers, It's me."

"Maggie, what are you doing here? I thought you went off in a cab."

"I did, but I had the cab driver drop me off in the Bronx, just on the other side of the river. I thought he might be a spy for Albert and the Bund. The cab was so easy to get. I told the cabby that I was staying with a girlfriend for the night. Then I took another cab right back here. I was worried about you. I saw them take you into the back room. I listened at the window. I heard you say that you would look into a murder. You're not going to kill someone, are you?"

I said, "Ah, sure, aren't you the one, to worry about me. Thank you, me dear. Now let's walk a few blocks west until we are out of Yorkville, and we'll grab a safe ride home. Where do you live anyway?"

"In Jackson Heights. It's a long car ride. I can take the train."

"Maggie, I'm going to see you to your door, me dear. You don't want me to be losing sleep worrying about you, now, do you?"

The ride to Queens cost a pretty penny, but knowing that we were all safe for the night was worth the expense. I took a train back to Manhattan. I sure wished I lived closer to Jackson Heights, but then I would be quite a bit away from Murphy's.

****

Saturday July 1, 1939
Dear Diary,
My heart is in my mouth. Blathers and I had something like a date. I went a little early and tried to make him jealous of this guy Albert. I don't know if it worked. Anyway, I thought Blathers might be headed for trouble, so I pretended to leave. Albert got me a taxi, but I didn't trust the taxi guy, so I had him drop me off just across the river in the Bronx. I told him I was going to stay with a girlfriend, in case he was going to report back to Albert. Then I got another cab and went back to the restaurant. I hung around outside so I would be there if trouble broke out. I listened at a

100

window in the back, and I heard them tell Blathers to kill someone. Then Blathers came out and I met him.

Now the good part. He insisted on bringing me home. We got a cab, and he let the cab go when we got to my place, and then he came to my door. I didn't know what to do, but I had just mustered up the courage to invite him in, when he said goodnight, turned on his heel, and took off. I know it is probably a sin, but I wish he had stayed.

Chapter 29

"They think I'm a killer. I guess I planted the idea that I came here from Ireland because I was wanted. They have assumed I was an assassin for the IRA. Now they want me to kill someone to prove I am worthy to belong to their organization."

Duff picked up the luger I had put on his desk. "Well, they gave you a pretty hefty weapon to do the job. What's your plan? Remember, they may just be using you for a patsy. You kill someone who is troublesome to them, and then you get caught. They get rid of you and another problem all at once."

"Sure, I've thought of that. I'm certainly not going to kill anyone. But think of this—suppose we clue in Fitzgerald and Higgins and set a trap. This might be the way for us to complete our primary mission, to catch the killer of the jeweler."

Duff said, "Okay, suppose I try to set up a meeting for around three this afternoon."

****

It was on to noon, and I was ready to grab a burger in Flushing. As I left Duff's office, Maggie said, "Blathers, can I talk to you for a minute?"

"Sure, me sweet, you can talk to me for hours. Why don't you let me buy you a burger in Flushing? You know, that place near the train tracks. We can take the train, the one-stop, or walk if you're up to it."

"Fine, let's walk. I need the exercise."

****

The occasional rumble of the Long Island Rail Road running by was no trouble because the burgers were so good. Maggie and I sat at a little table along the wall. We did all the small talk. I thanked her for her concerns of the night just passed. She thanked me for seeing her home. I commented on how nice her building was. She said she felt safe in the neighborhood. I offered to treat for lunch. She said I didn't have to pay for her lunch. I said it was my pleasure. We suspended our conversation to let a train rush by. When it was quiet again, I said, "So, Maggie, what was it you wanted to talk to me about?"

"It's our dear friend Albert. He phoned me this morning and asked me on a date. There is a big German party planned. You know, all the beer you can drink, all the sausage and sauerkraut you can eat, and an oomp-pa-pa band. I don't know what to do. I don't dislike Albert, but I don't agree with his allegiance to Hitler. Plus, I don't really like sausage, or sauerkraut, or loud music. On the other hand, I know that you are somehow investigating him and his pals. I don't want to mess up what you are doing. Should I go? Will it help your investigation?"

I smiled. I thought, this young lady is a fine young lady. "Oh, gee whiz, don't worry about messing up anything. Just tell him you can't go because you are engaged to be married to me."

"Is this a proposal?"

"Sure. For right now, it's a bit of a deceit, but you never know. It might turn to something more in the future, don't you see."

Now the poor girl was turning red. She stammered a wee bit, and finally said, "Why don't I just tell him I am seeing someone else, and he doesn't want me to go out with any other men."

I smiled at her. "Sure, it sounds fine to me. Now, let's finish up here. I have a meeting this afternoon with Duff and some others."

****

Shortly before three o'clock, Fitzgerald appeared in the office. Five minutes later, Higgins was shown in by one of our people on the front gate. Duff said, "Make yourselves as comfortable as possible, gents. Blathers has a story to tell you. I told them about my assignment from Kuhn and showed them the luger.

Higgins said, "Well, two things. First, let me make a phone call and get some extra men up to protect the Goldman house and guard Mrs. Goldman if she should go out. Next, let me borrow the gun. We can get a ballistics reading on it and see what happens."

I said, "Sure, that sounds good, but we also want to use this to help prove who really killed Goldman."

Higgins made his phone call. We all agreed this was an opportunity to solve the murder of the jeweler, so we concocted a plan. Higgins took the gun with him when he left, and then brought it back to me, personally, before five that afternoon. He cautioned me to keep the luger safe.

Chapter 30

That night I met with Kuhn and Albert in the back room of the Berghoff. I placed the luger on the long table in front of Kuhn, turned, and went to sit at the opposite end. "Now, I have looked the place over and assessed the risk. Sure, there is no way I can go up there and shoot that woman without being caught. There is a grand security system, and there are cops all over the place. I'll ask, did you take a look at the place before you sent me to be arrested? Did you think I didn't know what I was doing?" I put on a good act for the boys.

Kuhn glared at me. "I thought you were an experienced man at this type of activity."

"Don't you see, that's just it. I'm experienced enough to know when a job is a suicide job."

Kuhn regained his composure and quietly said, "You're nothing but a coward. Perhaps it's the Irish in you. We don't want anyone in our organization who is not fully committed to risking everything for the cause."

"Where I come from, we think it's important to live to fight another day."

At a nod from Kuhn, Albert stood up and put his hand on the back of my chair. I felt something hard and cool against the back of my neck. The luger had disappeared from the table. Kuhn went on. "Unfortunately, you now know too much about our operation. We can't let you just wander out of here."

I needed to play for a little time. "Faith, now, wait just one minute. If you're saying that if I don't kill the lady, you're going to kill me, then I'll kill the lady. Give me the gun."

Albert said, "I don't think so. You can't be trusted."

"Sure, now, if you don't give it to me, I'll take it." I stood quickly. Albert squeezed the trigger. The gun went click. I smacked Albert in the jaw and grabbed the gun while he was falling. Kuhn had jumped up and was pulling another gun out of a shoulder holster. I knew that one was loaded. I threw the luger at him and hit him in the neck. I then lifted my end of the table and pushed it over on top of the American führer. Behind me, the door smashed open, and Officer Higgins of the homicide squad barged in. "We have a report of illegal gambling going on here. Put your hands up and come with me." He apparently didn't see Kuhn or Albert, who were both hidden by the upturned table. I allowed Higgins to arrest me. Kuhn and Albert remained hidden by the table.

Chapter 31

July 8, 1939 was a Saturday. As night was falling, I sat next to Higgins in the front room of a house owned by a Mr. and Mrs. Peter Roth. We were looking across the street at the house of the widow Goldman. The neighborhood in the Bronx was made up of middle-class Dutch Colonial houses. Some had gabled roofs, some had gambrel roofs. Some had center entrances, and others had entrances set to the front left of the house. They all had driveways and garages, because no self-respecting resident of suburbia would be without an automobile, and this area of the Bronx was the finest example of suburbia in 1939. Each also had a concrete walkway to the front door.

One of the other features of all the houses was a line of windows looking onto the street. Since the Goldman house entrance was set to the side, all of the windows were in the living room. Higgins and I sat looking out the front of the Roths' house, which also had an entrance set to the side and a row of four windows in the living room looking out on the street.

The neighborhood was quiet. All the surrounding residents had been invited to a dinner party hosted by the New York Police Department at a midtown Manhattan hotel. There was one car parked in the driveway of the house next door to the Roth house.

As Higgins and I sat looking across the street,

waiting for darkness, we could see the silhouette of someone listening to her Zenith console radio. Either Lowell Thomas was saying "Good bye, everyone," or "Mister District Attorney" was in the middle of solving a murder, while a real murder was about to happen.

As soon as it was completely dark, a sleek car pulled up in front of the Goldman residence. There were two men in it. The driver kept the engine running while the passenger got out and headed for the front windows. When he was a few feet away, he pulled a gun from his belt and fired twice at the seated image.

Window glass shattered. The head of the seated figure split into several pieces of pine wood. The wig fell from the head as the remaining part of the dummy fell forward onto the floor.

At the sound of the shots, the car from the driveway next door backed into the street, red lights flashing and siren blaring, to block the getaway car. Higgins barked, "Go!" into his two-way radio, and police cars came roaring down the street from each direction. The gunman turned and saw the trap. He looked toward his getaway car, fired twice at his driver, dropped the gun, and ran toward the back yard of the next house.

Higgins and I ran to the getaway car, and there slumped over the steering wheel, with blood on his shirt and two neat holes in the side of his head, was my good friend from Yorkville, Albert.

****

Sunday July 9, 1939
Dear Diary,
So after leaving church this morning, I head to the Acropolis for breakfast as usual. The rule about not

eating after midnight if you are going to receive communion sure makes me starving by the time the nine o'clock Mass is over. I could go to the seven o'clock service, but I guess I'm too lazy.

In any event, the waitress gave me a cup of coffee, and while my pancakes and sausage are being made I start reading my paper. The sports section is all about Lou Gehrig Day at Yankee Stadium on the 4th and that young tennis player, Bobby Riggs, who won the Men's Championship at Wimbledon.

Then I turn to the local news and a story about an attempted murder the night before. There is a picture, and Blathers is in the background. Is he a murderer or was he murdered? He is just standing there. He doesn't look shot, and he doesn't look arrested. I decided I had better head for the office right after breakfast.

****

We gathered in Duff's office late on Sunday morning. Maggie joined in, as did our two Irish cop pals, Fitzgerald and Higgins. She had seen the picture of me at the murder scene in the paper. She was very upset. "Why didn't I know about what was going on? You could have been killed."

I just shook my head. "Maggie, the police were in control. We couldn't say anything to anyone." She pouted.

Duff asked, "So where do things stand?"

Higgins said, "Well, the assassin got away. He must have thought there was a trap, or else he is just a very cautious guy. He had a car parked on the next street over. By the time we got there he was long gone."

Duff said, "I'll bet he intended to kill Albert all along, and that's why he had a car waiting."

Fitzgerald chimed in, "I agree with Duff. Albert was to be shot so he would not squeal on the Bund if he was caught. That way we can't pin this on Kuhn and his bunch. Sure, they are crafty fellows."

Maggie said, "Certainly there must be something we can do."

I said, "I can testify that Kuhn wanted me to murder Mrs. Goldman."

Higgins scratched the back of his head. "I checked with the DA. He says it's just your word against Kuhn's. If he tries to prosecute Kuhn, it will just give the Nazis a chance to say they are being persecuted. They would love a chance to say their right to free speech is being violated by the authorities."

I said, "Sure, now, Mrs. Goldman is still in danger, then."

Higgins answered, "Mrs. Goldman is on an extended vacation. We have told her that we are trying our best to bring her husband's killers to justice. We stressed that we didn't want to lose her in the effort. She agreed with that. Where she is, even I don't know."

Duff and I looked at each other and shrugged our shoulders at the same time. Duff said, "Well, I guess we'll have to let the situation be as it is, for now."

Book Three: "Dimensions, Senses, Affections"
Chapter 32

Things started to slow down at the Fair after Labor Day. Once school got underway, the majority of visitors were school kids. And it wasn't just from grade schools; high schools and colleges brought classes often. One of the first groups to visit was a history class from Queens College, a neighbor on the outskirts of Flushing. The college was only two years old, but it was quickly developing a fine reputation. Several other groups from the New York-based colleges followed. The physics students were just as interested in television as they were in beer. Most of the grade school kids were only interested in the amusement rides. The high school kids were interested in each other. The major security functions were to make sure none of the little kids got injured on the amusement rides, make sure none of the teens disappeared into dark corners, and make sure the physics students didn't take home any of the parts of the exhibits.

It was around the middle of September that I got a letter from the lawyer Littlefield asking me to give him a call. I phoned the next day, and he told me it was time to start building the motel. He needed my signature on some documents. I was also needed to meet with the contractor to approve the plans for the building, like I know anything about building plans. Once again, all that was required was for me to sign a number of documents. Once again, I hesitated, considering that Littlefield represented a group of con men and women. Once again, I thought, What have I got to lose? the only thing I own that's of any value is my matched set of darts. I signed everything.

The building plans, which I gallantly approved, were interesting. The motel would be two stories, with twenty-eight rooms. On the ground floor, in the center of the structure, there was a sizable office where guests would check in. There was a full basement, but there were no detailed plans for what would be in the basement. Strangely enough, the plans did show stairs from the office to the basement, and also outside entrances to the basement at both ends of the building. I wondered what or who would be kept in the basement.

As business was completed, Littlefield patted my shoulder. "Now, Blathers, be sure and stop by from time to time to check on the progress of your building. You understand, of course, that when the building is complete, you will hire GJ Motel Management Company to run the day-to-day operations."

I understood that I was once again a pawn in this game against the Nazis. What I didn't understand was why I was needed and what would happen because I was involved.

Chapter 33

Each day as we approached the end of October and the date the Fair would close until next May, activity lessened. Finally, October 31 rolled around. It was time for a party. The entrance gates were all padlocked for the season. The only entrance still open was the rear entrance near the Security Office. This would remain open for two reasons. One was that security would be maintained during the winter, and the second was that we had to let the staff out. It was party time. At the magic hour, everyone gathered in the Beer Garden and finished off any beer that was left. Mr. Whalen made a speech thanking everyone for making the first year such a success.

Everyone said goodbye to everyone. I said goodbye to Maggie, and she kissed me on the lips. That was a surprise.

****

Wednesday November 1, 1939
Dear Diary,
I did it. I couldn't help myself. I kissed him. It was swell. He looked so surprised. Maybe I'll lose my job. He might tell Duff what happened, and Duff might think I'm too bold, or he might think I'm a distraction. Oh, gee, why did I do it? Was it because I might not see him for several months? Or maybe because I think I love him? Oh, gee, I can't believe I wrote that down. What

am I going to do for the next six months?

Duff said he would call me to come in from time to time to do some bookwork, but I'll bet it's at a time Blathers won't be there. I don't even know where he lives. Ah, but I do know where he goes to Mass on Sunday.

****

After the party I went to the pub to shoot some darts. I couldn't get the kiss out of my mind. Worst game I ever shot. I didn't sleep well, either. Well, I guess I won't be seeing her much over the winter. I know where she lives, but I don't think it would be good just to drop in uninvited. I know where she goes to church. Maybe I could bump into her at Mass. I could say I was going to the Fair site and her church was on the way, so I was only there because it was convenient for me.

****

Sunday December 3, 1939
Dear Diary,

I missed seeing Blathers so I went to Mass this morning at his church. I was going to say I was visiting a girlfriend who lived in the neighborhood, and it was convenient for me to go to Mass there. I would tell him that my girlfriend wasn't with me because she's Protestant. But he wasn't there.

****

I had to work anyway. So I went to her church. But she wasn't there. After work I took the LIRR to Bayside and walked to the construction site. It was a few miles, but I needed the exercise. It seems that, since I've had more time to hang around the pubs, I've put on a pound or two around the middle.

I was astonished at how much work had been done. It looked like the exterior would be finished soon so the workmen could move inside as the weather turned. I wondered what was going to happen when the place opened for business. Then I walked back to the railroad and took it into the city. Since I had walked about four miles, I decided I was entitled to a trip to Murphy's for a pint and a game or two of darts. I kept my darts behind the bar so they were available whenever I got a challenge. I seldom paid for my own pint.

****

On the following Tuesday the news came out. Fritz Kuhn was convicted of embezzling from the Bund. According to the afternoon papers, his two lieutenants, Gerhard Kunz and August Klaprrott, turned evidence of the embezzlement over to District Attorney Thomas E. Dewey. The story indicated that Kuhn had a lady friend and he supported her with Bund funds.

I was in the office late in the afternoon when Frieda called. "Oh, Blathers, Kuhn is going to jail. What a wonderful Hanukkah gift." I didn't know what Hanukkah was, so I asked. "It's a Jewish holiday that runs for eight days. Tomorrow is the first day of the celebration. It is a time of gift giving. The whole Jewish community will celebrate the jailing of Kuhn as one of the best gifts of the season."

I told Frieda I had visited the motel and was surprised at the progress, and then I wished her a happy holiday season. She said, "Blathers, I want to thank you for all your help."

I know it's terrible, but I couldn't help wondering if Frieda's thank-you was sincere, or was it just part of a con job, and I was the sucker. Oh, well, my only asset, my darts, was safe behind Murphy's bar.

Chapter 34

Time passed, but my thinking about Maggie didn't pass. Duff and I met two or three times a week. He had been relaxing and taking in New York. He said, "Last week I went to the Met for a Saturday matinee, *Boris Godunov* with Ezio Pinza. It was great. Then after, I had an early dinner at a little French café, Chez Marcelle. I have been enjoying New York, but I would like to go back to Chicago for Christmas and New Year's Eve." He asked if I would mind looking after things while he was gone. He has been so good about helping me to help my Jewish friends that I was glad to have a chance to do something for him. But when he'd packed his bag and I saw him get on the train at Grand Central, it occurred to me that it could be a very lonely holiday season for me. So I marched over to the subway and took the train to Jackson Heights.

When I got to the street where Maggie lived, I got cold feet in more ways than one. It was a bitter day, and it was a three-block walk to her building from the elevated station. My feet were freezing, and I realized I was about to call on a girl empty-handed. I ducked into a corner drug store and looked around for something appropriate. I would tell her I had stopped to bring her a little Christmas gift. They had some nice perfume, but that seemed a little bit intimate for the occasion, even though I must admit that I had intimacy in the back of

117

my mind.

There didn't seem to be anything appropriate, so I asked the proprietor for some advice. When I explained my situation, he said, "I think I understand. If I were you, I would go back to the corner and go right. About five doors down you'll find a very nice book store. A new best seller would be the thing, I think." He was right. I got a new copy of *The Yearling* for her, hoping she hadn't already read it. I walked back to her building with more confidence, rang her bell in the lobby, and heard a curt, "Who is it?"

"Hi, Maggie. 'Tis me, Blathers. I was on me way to work and wanted to stop off to see you. I have a small gift for you, a kind of Christmas present. But sure, if it isn't a good time, I can leave it here in the lobby, and you can get it when you next come down. Now, I don't want to intrude."

"Oh, no, no. Come right up. I'll buzz you in. You must be frozen, walking from the train. We can have some coffee, come right up. Oh, the buzzer." I heard the buzz and opened the door. Then I realized I didn't know which apartment was hers. Back to the phone.

"Hi..."

"Maggie, which apartment is yours?"

"Oh, 3C. On the third floor. Just come up to the third floor. Look for apartment C." She hung up, but I needed to be buzzed in again. I rang again. "What? Oh, the buzzer, the buzzer." The buzzer sounded again, and finally I was on my way to 3C.

****

Thursday December 21, 1939
Dear Diary,
Well, what a day. Blathers showed up at my door

with a gift, a beautiful copy of The Yearling. *I don't know how he knew I like to read. It must be part of the thing that is happening between us. Just this morning I was wondering how I could get in touch with him, and there he was on my doorstep. We had a pleasant cup of coffee together, but I had to go to my holiday job at Macey's, so we couldn't do anything but have coffee.*

He asked me what I was doing for Christmas. I told him I was going to go and visit my parents in Ithaca. He looked as disappointed as I felt. But I told him I would be back for New Year's Eve, and Dear Diary, we have a date.

Chapter 35

My date with Maggie was a grand success. There was dinner at Cousin Bernie's house. Then off to the local pub, Murphy's, to welcome in a new year and a new decade. Even though it wasn't the poshest place, and even though most of the folks were from the old country, and even though there was the threat of war on the horizon, we all had a lovely time. At midnight everyone kissed everyone, and I kissed Maggie for a bit of time more than was usually considered appropriate. I saw Maggie home, and we kissed for the second time that night. And being the gentleman that I am, I went back to Manhattan for the night.

Now that the holidays had passed, and Duff was back from his trip to Chicago, it was time to start preparing for the reopening of the Fair in May.

On Monday, February 5, we called Maggie back to work. She and I had agreed to keep the relationship that had blossomed since the first of the year out of our workplace. We were sure that Duff suspected something, but we made every effort to behave as we had the previous season.

The first step in preparation for the reopening was to send a letter to those we had hired the prior year, inviting them to let us know if they were available. Experienced folks were worth more, so we had persuaded Mr. Whalen to let us offer a raise to returning employees. Maggie got a raise too, but that was Duff's idea. It's a good thing, because she worked her lovely little fingers to the bone typing all those letters. I was thinking that it would be wonderful if someone invented a machine that would just copy the first letter. We could have Maggie type one without the name and address, make some copies, and then all Maggie would have to do is type in the correct name and address on each copy. I told this to Maggie, and she said there was a chap who lived near her in Jackson Heights trying to build a machine like that. Maybe some of the world of tomorrow isn't at the Fair.

As we got responses, we began to plan how best to use folks. Some wanted to work only the day shift, and some wanted to work only the late shift. Duff had purchased a pad of spreadsheets, and he would make lists on it. As things began to develop, he went to the stationery store a second time and bought a box of erasers.

We were deep in our planning when we had a visit from Officer Higgins of the Homicide Squad. When he strolled in at around ten a.m. one Friday, I had the feeling things weren't good. He wasn't the type to stop by for coffee, a doughnut, and casual conversation. "Can I have a chat with you, Blathers? Sure, it's about your building project, and another death, which I think is a murder."

"My building project? And oh, gee whiz, a murder? What murder?"

"A fellow was found in the basement this morning. On the surface, it seems he fell through an opening from the second floor right through to the basement. I guess there is to be a stairway from the basement to the second floor, because there is a large open area on both the first and second floors."

I said "Faith, doesn't that sound like an accident to me."

Higgins scratched his head. "Perhaps it's supposed to look like an accident, and then again, perhaps it's not. There's not enough blood on the floor where the body was found, and there's a big gash in the side of his head, but there isn't anything I can see that would have caused it. No, I think the guy was killed someplace else and thrown into the basement. I also think the killers were either very stupid or they wanted us to know it was a murder."

Duff sat listening. Then he said, "So why are you here, Officer Higgins? You can't think that Blathers had anything to do with it."

Higgins shook his head. "I don't know who has anything to do with it, do I, now. I'm just looking into the possibilities. We haven't even identified the body yet. So, Blathers, I'd like you to come down to the morgue to see if you know the fellow."

I agreed to look at the victim, and we went out the security entrance and got into Higgins' car.

The Queens County morgue was in Jamaica. It was only a fifteen-minute ride from Flushing. I had been in morgues before, during my training with the police. They all smell the same.

The attendant rolled out a table. Apparently the autopsy had not been done yet. He pulled back the sheet, and there, cold and white on the table, was the man who had pretended to be Jacob Stern's son and Rhonda Rosen's brother. He now had blond hair and a mustache, but there was no mistake; it was him.

Chapter 36

Higgins asked, "Do you recognize him?"

"Oh, gee whiz, yes and no."

Higgins turned red with frustration and yelled, "What do you mean? Yes or no?"

"Oh, gee whiz, take it ease now, Officer. I mean I have seen him before, but I don't know who he really is."

Apparently, this response only increased the policeman's frustration. I wanted to explain to him, but once again I was in a situation where I would have to either blow the whistle on Frieda Ullman's operation or make up a story. I decided to make up a story.

"Officer Higgins, before you have a stroke, let me explain." Now I had to think fast. "I was introduced to this fella some time ago at a bar in the city. I think he was an actor, but I'm not sure. And, I might have had a pint or two at the time, because the whole thing is a little fuzzy, if you get my meaning." I wanted to talk to Frieda before telling Higgins anything more. "I'll tell you what, though. Give me about three hours, and I think I'll be able to find out all you want to know about the poor fella."

"Why don't I go along with you while you make your inquiries?"

"Oh, gee whiz, no, no. The folks I'm going to see will confide in me only if I'm alone. It's kind of like confession, if you know what I mean. But in this case, I'll be able to tell you all I find out. After all, I'm not a priest."

Before he could say anything more, I hotfooted it through the door.

****

The bus ran right down Kissena Boulevard, from Jamaica straight to Flushing. I was back in the office in less than a half hour. I found Mr. Littlefield's phone number. He was in. "Mr. Littlefield, this is Blathers. Is this a party line?"

"No, you can talk. All the other parties on the line are me." He laughed.

He stopped laughing when I told him what was going on. "I'll call Frieda right away. How soon can you be here?"

"Sure, I'm on me way now. Twenty minutes."

****

Frieda looked as good as ever. Blonde hair set off her slightly darker complexion. The contrast was absorbing, amazing, and adorable, all at the same time. Lawyer Littlefield looked like he always did. The same blue three-piece suit, the same white shirt, and the same red tie. He sat behind his desk with his hands folded over his ample belly. He said, "Now, Blathers, please start from the beginning for Miss Ullman."

I didn't know if the murdered man was really Frieda's brother, so I asked, "Oh, gee whiz, you remember the fella that said he was your brother back when you were, shall I say, dealing with Whalen—was he really your brother?"

"No, but he is a good friend and an important part of our operation. Why do you ask?"

"Sure, I'm sorry to have to tell you, but he has been killed."

She looked like she didn't believe me, but then tears rolled down the beautiful lady's cheeks. Finally, she choked back some sobs and said, "He was not my brother, and he was not my lover, but he was as close to me as a brother or a lover would be. What has happened?"

I told the rest of the story and then asked both Frieda and Littlefield what I should tell Officer Higgins.

Littlefield moved a bit in his chair and said, "We have to protect Frieda and the organization. How about you tell them you have talked to some actor friends, and you think he is an out-of-work actor. You were told that his real name is Harold Berger. His parents live in the Bronx. His father's name is Harold Berger too. That should provide enough for the police to work with. You don't know your actor friends that well, so you only know their first names or nicknames. You're sorry, but that's all you could find out."

"Okay, I'll give it a go, and we'll see what happens. As me sainted mother used to say, what have we got to lose."

Frieda said, "That might keep the police off our backs for a while, but I think we need to find out why Harold was killed, who killed him, and why he was dumped at the motel."

Chapter 37

I went back to Flushing, stopped into the police station, and asked Boyle how I could get in touch with Higgins. "Sure, that won't be a problem, now, will it. He is in the boss's office at this very moment. I am quite sure it will be fine if you just go and knock on the door." I did as Boyle indicated, and Higgins opened the door to let me in. I sat down and told him and Fitzgerald what Littlefield had told me to say.

Higgins said, "Well, now, that's not very much."

"Sure, I am sorry, but that's all I could find out, now, isn't it. At least it's a lead."

"Yes, we will have to break the bad news to his parents, and perhaps they can give us some more information. I wonder, though, how come the body was found where it was."

I said, "Now, aren't I thinking the same thing meself."

Higgins said, "That's the second unsolved murder involving your property. Do you think that's just a coincidence?"

My property? Yes, I kept forgetting what a big business man I was. "The first body was found before it was my property, so you can't blame me for that one. This one has been found while the property is under construction. Sure, ask the contractor what happened, not me. I'm not over there pounding nails, now, don't you know."

Fitzgerald said, "We understand, Blathers, and we are much obliged for your help."

Higgins said, "Humph," and went away, but he did not seem to be a very happy man.

****

I walked back to the office, going in the back entrance, the only one open while the fair was shut down. Duff was there. He wanted all the details. "Blathers, my friend, we need to get to the bottom of both killings, or you and your friends, including Miss Ullman, are going to end up in jail."

Book Four: "Every man must play a part."
Chapter 38

It looked to me like it was time I, Duff, took a more active role in the activities of Blathers and the group of—what were they, con men or soul savers? I guess it was a question about what is legal and what is moral. Let's see. Laws are made by men, men who are in power. They are not always good men. Moral issues seem to come from a higher power. My dad always taught me to do what was right. I guess my dad would want me to become a con man along with Blathers, Maggie, and Frieda Ullman.

The first step was for the four of us to get together and find out what we needed to do to solve the murders and protect the operation. I asked Blathers to arrange something.

****

We met at the Fair office. It was nice of Mr. Whalen to provide a place for the meeting and to pay three of us for our time. I'm not sure we addressed the moral issues of using the Fair's resources for other than Fair business. Perhaps we thought Whalen would be happy to contribute to a good cause. After all, he had already given them $25,000. Anyway, so I wouldn't feel too guilty, I paid out of my own pocket for a new pad of large paper, suitable for making lists, the grease pencil, and the easel that I set up to hold the pad.

This was a pad that would not be kept in the office.

As it developed, Frieda would take it with her. Too many police, FBI, and Fair employees were in and out of the place.

On the second page—I always kept the first page blank to foil any casual observer who might interrupt us—I wrote:

OUR TASKS

1. Find out who is killing people, so that none of us get accused.

2. Find out how to best fund the organization without going to jail.

Blathers said, "Now, folks, don't worry about the lists. Isn't it just Duff's way of keeping us from getting off the track in our thinking. He always makes lists, don't you know."

Frieda, the good lady, said, "I think it's an excellent idea. Let's get started. Let's tackle the first item first. As for the second matter, I think we will have to involve our lawyer, Mr. Littlefield, to some extent. Of course, he doesn't want to know that any of our activities are not within the letter of the law. After all, he is an officer of the court. The way we handle that is to not tell him what we have done, but tell him what we have planned. If he says don't do that, it's against the law, we are more careful about being caught."

I liked Frieda. She had a bold way about her. I asked if she knew what the recent victim was doing when he was killed.

"He was selling books."

I said, "Selling books, what books?"

"Well, they were signed copies of *Mein Kampf*. There are thousands of copies of that horrible book out there, and they are cheap, but not many signed by Hitler himself. They are expensive. Harold had somehow acquired a bunch of signed copies. He dyed his hair blond, grew a mustache, had a few fake tattoos put on his arms, and went up to Yorkville, pretending he recently came from Germany. He had a wonderful German accent, and, because of the autograph, had no problem getting top dollar for the books. It's my guess he just sold one too many."

I was still confused. "Where did he get the signed copies?"

"There are people in our group who have many talents. Like Harold, who could change from a skinny Jew to a robust Nazi without much difficulty. You remember his big nose? Gentiles always think that if you have a big nose you are a Jew. It went in the trash with other items of used makeup. If we can change a person like that, we can change a book to something valuable without any trouble. We have a lot of ways of acquiring the cash we need."

It dawned on me, another con job. I guess there are things I don't want to know and questions I shouldn't ask. I wrote on another page of the pad:

Harold Berger was working on the Upper East Side of Manhattan as a salesman before he was killed.

Blathers asked Frieda, "What was the relationship of Goldman, the jeweler, to your group?"

"He was a benefactor, not an actor, although he would occasionally invest in a play in the Village. He was at the cabins to make a donation, to help us finance our moving to a new location. You remember, the FBI was hot on our trail. He gave us the money, and we left the cabins. He was looking around after we left. I wouldn't be surprised if he was thinking of buying the property. Anyway, it must be that before he left the place, someone attacked him. How anyone knew he was there, I have no idea. Maybe he was killed just because he was there."

I asked, "Do you think he was killed just because he was a Jew?"

"It's hard to say. Maybe he was a Jew that was just in the wrong place at the wrong time. Maybe the Bund wanted to frame us for murder."

Blathers added, "Remember, now, the Bund wanted me to kill his wife. Certainly that must mean they probably had something to do with Mr. Goldman's killing."

I said, "I somewhat agree with Frieda. But I think that it was an attempt to set Blathers up for the murder of Goldberg. Remember, you knew too much. If you had even gone close to Mrs. Goldberg, they would have shot you the way they shot that guy Albert, and then when they shot her, they would put the gun in your hand. To the cops it would be case closed. I bet the cops may think that Albert killed Goldberg, and that's probably why we haven't heard more from Brown and his pal from the FBI."

Blathers went into his thinking mode, stroking his chin. "So, now, doesn't it seem to me that Fritz Kuhn doesn't mind a little killing, particularly of Jews, and he has someone who does the killing for him."

I said, "If that's the case, we will have a tough time pinning anything on him. No one is ever going to admit that Kuhn ever ordered the assassination of anyone."

Maggie finally spoke up, "Yes, but if we pinned it on the actual killer, then maybe Kuhn would have a hard time getting someone else to do his dirty work."

I said, "You're assuming that Goldman's killer and Harold's killer are the same person."

Frieda said, "Since both were connected to the Bayside property, I think we should work on that assumption."

I made some additional entries on the list and asked, "How are we going to catch him then?"

OUR TASKS

1. Find out who is killing people, so that none of us get accused.

2. Find out how to best fund the organization without going to jail.

3. For (1) It appears that the killings were authorized by Kuhn.

4. We believe that the same person did both the killings.

5. If we nab the actual killer, we may be able to inhibit the Bund's ability to employ other assassins.

Frieda smiled. "We'll set a trap. Give me and my friends a day or two to think of something. We're good at this kind of thing."

Chapter 39

One week had passed when Frieda finally called and asked if we could meet again. That afternoon, we gathered to hear what she and her group had planned. She began, "Since we have no idea who or where our killer is, we need some bait to bring him out of hiding."

I asked, "What do you have in mind for bait?"

Frieda cleared her throat and looked at the floor. "Blathers."

Maggie immediately jumped from her chair. "What do you mean?"

Frieda said, "Well, here is the plan. You can accept it or reject it. First of all, we are not going to get the killer to show himself if the only target we provide for him is a cardboard box. The bait has to be a living person. They, the bad guys, already know Blathers, so we won't have to introduce them to anyone new. In addition, Blathers is already a property developer. Since, in our plan, the bait needs to be a property developer or owner, Blathers is the best choice. There is, of course, some risk, but I'll bet we can mitigate that to a great extent. I'm relying on the experience of the team of Blathers and Duff to deal with the safety issues."

I said, "We'll see about that when we hear the meat and potatoes. Go on."

"We think that one of the great goals of the Bund,

and one of the ways they keep their followers happy, is to keep Yorkville white and Christian. They do that by intimidating landlords, but what will they do if there is a landlord that won't be intimidated?"

Blathers said, "They'll murder the poor bastard, won't they, both to get rid of him and use him as an example to the others, and isn't that the truth."

Frieda went on, "Exactly, and who will they send to do the job? Our boy."

Blathers said, "I don't mind being the bait, but I don't own any property in Yorkville."

"As it happens, there is a building on West 85th Street. Mr. Littlefield has used his magic to arrange for the property to be put up for sale, and to be sold to you. He didn't ask and we didn't tell him why we wanted it. Once again, all you have to do is sign the papers and wait. We understand there are currently two vacant apartments. As soon as the deal is closed and you take over management, we will see that the first applicants are a Black family and a Jewish family. It won't be long before the tenants run to the Bund complaining. Then the action will start."

Maggie continued to protest. "It's too dangerous for Blathers. We might catch the killer, but Blathers will be dead. No, no, it's too, too risky."

I said, "It is unlikely that the assassin will strike during the daylight hours, so I think that by the use of one or two of our best men from here, and some of the newfangled body armor that is being developed, we can protect our bait."

Maggie asked, "Where are you going to get body armor?"

"There's a company in Chicago that our agency

there has worked for off and on. I'm sure they would be willing to field test some of their prototypes. We'll only use the kind that we think is going to work, and then Blathers can become rich and famous by advertising for them."

Blathers laughed. Frieda chuckled. Maggie frowned.

*****

Wednesday, February 14, 1940
Dear Diary,

Blathers and I had a Valentine's date tonight. I guess maybe it was our first real date. The other first date was on New Year's Eve, dinner at Cousin Bernie's and shooting darts in a pub. I'm not counting that as a real date even though there was some kissing, and he did see me home, but he didn't stay. I guess I don't have to count that as our first real date, even though he was sweet the whole evening.

We have also had breakfast together after Mass on a couple of Sundays. We got that mix-up thing, of him being at my church while I was at his, straightened out.

But this time it was Valentine's and much more like what I would call a real date. It was really swell. He took me to dinner at a restaurant that had cloth tablecloths. The waiters were polite and wore black bowties. We had a lovely dinner, and some delicious wine.

I think a real relationship could develop, except he will probably get killed if that Frieda has anything to do with it. I wish she would get on with her business and leave Blathers alone.

Chapter 40

The body armor arrived within a week of my conversation with my contacts in Chicago. We had a tailor measure Blathers and sent all the measurements to the maker of the armor. It fit him perfectly, but it added to his size. We had to buy him some larger clothes to fit over the armor. Frieda wanted to have the stuff after we were through with it. It would make skinny guys look fatter. I guess somewhere there was a stockpile of stuff that could change anyone's appearance.

We also wanted to test it to see if it really worked. Instead of putting it on Blathers and shooting at him, which was the first thought of Tony and Ralph, the two fellows we selected to help us in the caper, we built a dummy and blasted away at it. The dummy got a few dents, but none of the bullets penetrated the armor. This was good news, but we still wanted to plan so that we could nab our guy without a shot being fired. I also got measured and got a set of the same armor for myself.

I filled Tony and Ralph in on our plan, to the extent that they needed to know. They were men I'd recruited from Chicago to work at the Fair. They were guys who were not likely to do anything that would tip off Whalen to the fact we were doing more than watching the Fair, and since they were from out of town, it was unlikely they had any connection to anyone in the

Bund. We talked about getting some body armor for each of them, but they said they wouldn't wear it. They thought it would slow them down if they had to act fast.

So we had our team together. The next step was to travel up to Yorkville and see the building. We each went separately, so we wouldn't call attention to ourselves, and then met to discuss the layout later at my office. Blathers joined us. Frieda didn't need to be there, and Maggie wouldn't come because she didn't like the whole setup. I wasn't sure what was going on between her and Blathers, but she was sure he was going to be killed. Just let me say that in the past year I had become somewhat attached to Blathers myself, but of course not in the same way Maggie had. Even though he and I each have completely different personalities, I had started to look on him as a close friend. If I'd thought he was in danger, I wouldn't have gone through with the plan either.

****

The building was a six-story brick structure. There were five apartments on each floor. One elevator serviced the upper floors. Of course, there was a stairway that opened onto each floor. There was an apartment in the basement for the superintendent. He also served as janitor. We met with him, an old German guy with a bald head, a double chin, and a white goatee. English was not his best language, but that didn't matter because almost every tenant spoke some German. He said his name was Stan. I said that I thought Stan was a Polish name. He said he had a Polish mother. He shook hands with Blathers and me like we were his long-lost brothers. He wanted us to be sure to understand that he would be quite happy to stay in his current position.

Blathers asked to see the vacant apartments. Stan showed us one on the second floor near the stairway and one on the fifth floor at the rear of the building. We then looked around outside. There were fire escapes for all the apartments running down from the roof to a suspended ladder at the first floor. Stan pointed out that there were some clotheslines extending from some windows to others, and that some of the tenants dried their laundry on the roof. He said there were some washing machines and a laundry tub in the basement, adjacent to his apartment. He shook his head. If we got the gist of what he was trying to tell us, the limited laundry facilities led to disputes among some of the lady tenants. It appeared that was a time when Stan made sure his door was closed.

We returned to Stan's apartment in the basement, and he showed us how tenants gained entry to use the laundry facilities and to dispose of trash that wouldn't fit down the garbage chute. There was also an entrance at the back of the building and a large window that was used, according to Stan, "fer da coal ta comes in." The coalbin was adjacent to Stan's abode on the other side from the laundry, directly across from the furnace. The one advantage to Stan's apartment was that there was always plenty of heat.

The things the members of our team were interested in were the ways someone could get into the building, and the ways somebody could get out. Tony pointed out that, "In addition to all the doors, windows, and ladders, it wouldn't be too hard for someone to jump from the building next door to the roof of this building. It's going to be hard to secure the place."

I said, "We only want to secure someone's exit, not

his entry."

Blathers said, "You mean, after he has killed me."

Chapter 41

Toward the end of February, the deal closed, and Blathers became owner of the building as of March 1st. Littlefield's office had prepared and sent a notice to the tenants saying that as of that date they should send a check for their rent to Blathers, Inc. at his address in Great Neck. The notice also stated that, realizing some tenants would want to pay in cash, it was arranged that a representative of the landlord would be in the building lobby between ten a.m. and twelve noon on the first Saturday of each month. At that time, the representative would receive cash payments and discuss any concerns of the tenants.

On the first Saturday of March, I accompanied Blathers to the building to collect the rents. I was along with him because Blathers was uncertain about what might happen, and how much cash he might collect. I would have insisted on going with him even if he hadn't asked. There was no sense in taking chances.

All the tenants were anxious to meet the new landlord. Even if they had mailed a check, they stopped by to shake hands with Blathers. He assured each of them that Stan would be on the premises, and that he himself would be there the first Saturday of each month to make sure all was well. They all went away happy. That was soon to change.

Noon arrived, and the smell of German cooking in

the building soon seeped into the lobby. Blathers said, "Let's go over to the Berghoff Tavern for some lunch. These smells are making me hungry."

I agreed, and Blathers said, "I have to talk to Stan before we go." So we descended to the basement, where Stan was standing in the doorway of his apartment. "How vas da morning, sir?"

"It was very nice, sure now, Stan. I have come to tell you we are definitely keeping you on." Stan's face changed from a concerned frown to a big smile. "And it's not only that, we are increasing your monthly salary by five dollars." Stan almost exploded with joy. He pumped Blathers' hand until I thought his arm would become disconnected. Finally Blathers said, "Sure, now, we need to get the vacant units rented, don't we, so we can pay you on a regular basis. This afternoon at two o'clock a lovely family with two children will stop by. Please show them the larger apartment on the fifth floor."

"I vill I vill, da'll love it, you bet." Stan started shaking hands with Blathers again. Then he started on me. After two wild pumps, I smiled and pulled my hand away.

Blathers and I grinned at Stan, waved, and turned toward the stair to the first floor. Stan was still waving and bowing as we reached the top of the stairway and headed for some sauerbraten, a beer for Blathers, and some iced tea for me.

****

After lunch we went back to the Fair office. At about two-thirty, the phone rang. It was Frieda. I heard Blathers say, "Oh, gee whiz, I'm not surprised. Tell them to meet me in front of the building at exactly four o'clock. Tell them not to be early, for their own safety, and to leave the children home. I'll meet them there."

He hung up. "Oh, gee whiz, Stan wouldn't show the apartment because the family was Black. Now is the time to demonstrate that I don't care, don't you know. I'll show them the place this afternoon, and the whole neighborhood will be up in arms before they have their lovely supper."

I said, "I'll go with you and get Tony to meet us there."

Chapter 42

It was a big risk, violating an unwritten rule. Just the presence of a Black family in the neighborhood was enough to cause violence. In this neighborhood, maintaining an ethnic population was on the same level as attending church, whether one was Catholic or Lutheran. As a safeguard, I had Blathers call his cousin Bernie and ask him to park his cab on the street behind the 85th Street building. We got Tony to meet Bernie and make sure our prospects could get safely to the cab and away if it was necessary make a hasty escape.

We arrived at the building about fifteen minutes early and waited in the lobby. One or two tenants went in and out, and they nodded greetings to us. They were apparently quite satisfied that Stan had prevented what was, in their minds, racial contamination to the building, yet they weren't sure how the appearance of Black people happened in the first place. At exactly four, the front door opened and the Black couple entered the lobby. Blathers greeted them with a hearty handshake and introduced me as his business associate. I guess, under these circumstances, I wasn't his boss. Those tenants who were passing in and out at the time started to figure out that Blathers was not concerned about the racial purity of the place.

Apparently Blathers' advice had been followed and the decision had been made not to involve any children, which was definitely a good idea. I must say they were a handsome couple. He was at least six feet tall, with an athlete's physique. She had a radiant smooth black skin and a well-dressed very shapely body.

The couple introduced themselves. "Good afternoon, I'm Charles Robinson, and this is my wife, Glenda." He chuckled. "She was named long before *The Wizard of Oz* was produced."

As Blathers was saying, "Let me show you the apartment," a tenant got off the elevator. The tenant stepped into the lobby, and Blathers said, "Good afternoon," with a smile, and ushered the Robinsons into the elevator. It looked like getting the couple into the building would not be difficult. Getting them out might be a different matter.

In the apartment, Charles said, "Just so we are clear, we do not intend to rent the apartment. We are friends of Frieda Ullman and are here at her request, you understand."

Blathers said, "Sure, don't I know that, and don't I really appreciate the risk you are taking just being here. Mr. Duff and I are security people from the World's Fair. Did Frieda tell you why we are doing this?"

Glenda said, "We know about Frieda's organization. We are not regular members, but we certainly sympathize with her and her people. From time to time we help out as needed. She told us there might be some danger, but that she trusted you. If she trusts you, we trust you."

Blathers said, "As me sainted mother would say, you folks are a lovely couple."

I said, "Let's get you out of here. Blathers, you stay here with the Robinsons, and I'll go scout out the situation downstairs."

Charles smiled. "You be careful yourself, and by the way, our names aren't really Robinson, and we aren't really married, yet." He grinned at Glenda. "I hope someday." The look in Glenda's eye caused him to stop.

I said, "You can explain who you really are when we are safely away. I'll be back in a jiffy."

****

I took the stairs to the lobby, opened the door, and peeked in. At least fifteen people were gathered there. Three or four of the men were handling baseball bats. I closed the door slowly and returned to the fifth floor.

"We can't use the elevator to the lobby. I suggest we go down the stairs to the basement, out the back basement door, and down the back alley. One of our men and Blathers' cousin Bernie are waiting with a cab on the next street."

We set out down the stairs and all was clear until we reached the basement. Stan was there. Blathers went up to him. "Hi, Stan! Don't worry about renting the fifth-floor unit. It's taken." He kept walking forward until Stan backed into his living room.

While Blathers kept Stan blocked, the Robinsons—or whoever they were—and I went out the back door and up the back steps to the alley. We found Bernie and our man Tony waiting. Tony stayed on the sidewalk to make sure no one was following us, while the rest of us got in the car. "Bernie, these are my friends. Drive around the block once. Blathers should be right behind us."

We drove around once, and there was no Blathers. We drove around again, and there was no Blathers.

Even on our third trip we came up without Blathers, and the man we'd left on the back street had disappeared, too. "Bernie, drive past the front of the building." We drove down 85th Street. We could see there were still people in the lobby of the building. Some were even out on the street in front. In my wildest dream, I didn't think there would be this much of a commotion. But even with all the people that were there, there was no Blathers. Once more around the block, once more down 85th, no Blathers and no Tony.

"Bernie, pull over and let me out. Take these folks wherever they want to go, and meet me at the Fair office. When I get there, I'll pay you." I didn't want to say *if I get there*.

Chapter 43

I ran back down the alley, down the steps to the building's basement, and yanked open the door. It was quiet. The door to Stan's room was ajar and some light seeped out. I pushed it open slowly and saw Blathers sitting in an old Morris chair with the stuffing pushing out of the holes in the cushions, while Stan sat on an upturned milk crate.

Blathers looked up. "Ah, Duff. Now did our friends get off safely?"

"Yes, they did, but I was worried about you. I thought you would be right behind us."

"Sure, there was no need for that, now, was there. I needed to have a chat with my man, Stan, here. He needed to know that there would be folks by to look at the apartment on the second floor. And, sure, didn't he ask me if they are white. I assured them that they are. Apparently, Stan thinks Black folks are a bit inferior to him, and he doesn't like to be associated with them."

Stan said, "Da are messy. Da all lie, and got bugs. Besides, da got kids, vere vood da go ta school? Der's no Black school round here."

"Sure, if that's what you think, Stan, then won't we just send white folks for you to show apartments to. But that doesn't mean that some Black folks won't move in. The folks for the second floor will be here later this week. Come on, Duff, let's go over to the Berghoff and have a beer. Oh, I forgot. You'll be wanting tea. Well, at least we'll see if the story of our scandal has reached the folks we want to have know about it."

I followed Blathers as we climbed the stairs to the lobby. There were still five or ten tenants there. Blathers said, "Good afternoon, folks. Are you having a little party, now?" One man holding a baseball bat stepped into Blathers' path. "Ah, so you're off to a ball game. Isn't that grand, now, but a little chilly for baseball this time of year, I'd think." He slowly pushed the man aside with a wave of his arm and went out the door. I followed, hard on his heels.

Outside, Tony waited on the sidewalk. He had his hand inside his coat. Blathers said, "Ah, Tony, me boy, thank God you don't need to reach any deeper in your coat. Them boys' bark is worse than their bite. Will you join us for a beer? We're going to find out if we offended folks enough today."

****

At the Berghoff, we were met at the door by the owner. "We're not sure we want your trade."

I said, "News travels fast."

Blathers asked, "And why is that, now?"

"We heard what kind of a landlord you are."

"Oh, gee whiz, what kind is that?"

"You know. I don't have to spell it out for you." The owner started pushing Blathers toward the door. Several other patrons left their stools and headed for the fracas.

Then, suddenly, Fritz Kuhn was on the scene. "It's okay, Schultz. I believe Mr. Blathers realizes he has made a mistake, and he will not make that same mistake again. Come on and sit with me, Blathers, and let me meet your friends."

"Ah, if it isn't Mr. Kuhn, himself. It's okay, Mr. Kuhn. We'll find another place to drink."

We went to an Irish bar a short way downtown. They purveyed excellent tea and, according to Blathers and Tony, a lovely pint.

Chapter 44

Back at the office, Maggie said we had another call from Frieda. Blathers called her back. She wanted to know how we made out with the Robinsons. I said, "Didn't they say their name wasn't really Robinson?"

Maggie overheard me and questioned, "They were imposters?"

Blathers paused, looked at Maggie, put his hand over the phone, and said, "Maggie, they were actors. They changed their name to protect the innocent."

The conversation continued. Blathers assured Frieda that we all got away safe, and that the leaders of the Bund were getting the message. I thought I heard her laugh when he told her how we had snubbed Fritz Kuhn. After Blathers finished recounting the whole adventure, he listened for a few minutes. I heard him say, "What is a Hasidic Jew?"

When he finished the call, he said that Frieda was sending a very orthodox Jewish couple to meet Stan and see the apartment on Wednesday. "She said there would be no mistaking that they are Jewish. I guess we will wait and see how Stan and the neighborhood react to that."

****

Wednesday arrived, and Blathers made the same arrangements with Cousin Bernie. Cousin Bernie was getting expensive, but if we trapped a killer, we felt someone would reimburse us. In any event, it was a necessary precaution to make sure that none of Frieda's people would get injured.

Blathers and I were both in the lobby when the couple arrived. They were clearly Jews. I had seen folks dressed like this in parts of Brooklyn. Stan ran forward and yelled, "You folks in da vong place!"

Blathers said, "Now, Stan, they are white, you know."

Stan shook his head and said, "Der gonna be trouble," and went off to his basement hideout.

Stan was right. There was an angry gang forming on the street. I said, "Blathers, no time for any more show. Let's all get out the back way. You two follow us." Within minutes we were safely in Bernie's cab. Tony had been stationed with the cab to head off any unexpected trouble there. Ralph mingled with the fuming bunch in front of the apartment building. His job was to report on what he heard and saw. Tony and Ralph were left behind. We headed to Mr. Littlefield's office in Great Neck. Cousin Bernie was getting very rich.

In Great Neck, Frieda greeted us, and the actors set aside some of their clothing. The man removed his hat and some curls came with it. It turned out the couple weren't Jewish at all. Theater people!

****

Friday March 13, 1940
Dear Diary,
Well, we got through an exciting week and, guess what, Dear Diary, Blathers is still alive. I have kind of been put on the sidelines since I protested so much about the plan to make Blathers the bait to catch a

killer. They got two of the guys to help them. It must be that only men can be put in danger. Ugh, men. But I know that Blathers, Mr. Duff, and some of Frieda Ullman's friends have been in danger before.

Frieda Ullman—ugh! She thinks she's the bee's knees. Well, we'll see. Oh, I know both Blathers and Mr. Duff think she is doing a wonderful thing, helping people who might be killed in Europe. And I know the Nazis are not very nice to a lot of people, but I wonder if that is our problem. So many people want us to get involved in the war over there, but golly, why should American boys go over there and get killed? I just don't get it.

Anyway, St. Patrick's Day is next week. I wonder what Blathers has planned, and I wonder if his plans include me. I guess I hope so.

Chapter 45

As it turned out, Blathers had some great plans for St. Patrick's Day. He invited not only Maggie but me as well to have corned beef and cabbage at his local pub, Murphy's. He assured me the place made some of the finest tea in the world. I met Maggie on the Jackson Heights IRT platform at six, and we traveled together to Manhattan to meet Blathers. He had a table set aside for us where we could see the entertainers. The Daily Brothers played a variety of instruments including guitar, banjo, and, of course, the fiddle. The playlist was made up of standard Irish tunes. I didn't know most of them, but our Irish host and Maggie, his second-generation Irish lady friend as well as our secretary, were able to sing along when appropriate They really sang loudly to the chorus of "The Black Velvet Band"—

Her eyes, they shone like diamonds.
I thought her the Queen of the land.
And her hair hung over her shoulder,
Tied up with a black velvet band.

The food was wonderful and, as promised, the tea was of the highest order. Blathers reminded me that in Ireland most people drink tea instead of coffee. Apparently, the ale was of the best quality too. A great deal of it was being consumed all around us. Maggie had a few pints, and Blathers had one or two himself. But then he explained, "'Tis a night when a great many folks lose control of their drinking. Then, sure, isn't it a night when it's a good idea to maintain control of yourself. Now, then, my advice is that we should get out of here early, before the fighting starts."

We took Blathers' advice and, after some delicious apple pie for dessert, called for the bill at around eight p.m. Blathers insisted on treating both Maggie and me. "Sure, haven't the two of you been very helpful to me and to the folks I have been working with. This is just my way of showing how much you both are appreciated." We thanked him, he paid the bill at the bar, handed a dollar bill to our waitress, and we went out onto the street.

From a nearby dark doorway, two goons stepped out and blocked our path. "Good evening, Mr. Blathers." I could see that one guy had a blackjack in his hand, and the other was wearing brass knuckles. "Have you had a nice evening up to now?" One of them pushed Blathers in the chest, and the other pointed to Maggie and me. "We are only interested in speaking with Mr. Blathers. You two would do yourselves a favor if you hurried down the street right now."

Blathers stepped in front of Maggie and me. "Easy, lads. You know this isn't your neighborhood, don't you, now."

"It's about neighborhoods we want to talk to you. It's about keeping certain types out of our neighborhood."

I said, "By the looks of it, you didn't come just to talk."

Maggie started to fumble in her purse. Blathers

knew what she was looking for. "Now, Maggie, there's no need for that. If you would just be so kind as to step into the pub and tell them folks I have a spot of trouble out here."

Maggie dashed to the door, flung it open, and yelled, "Help!" The two hooligans had started to push Blathers against the wall of the building. When they saw what was happening, they stopped in their tracks. The doorway filled with men from the bar, well prepared for a fight. I heard one of the thugs yell, and I saw a dart sticking in his arm just above where he once held the blackjack. The other one turned and started to run away, but he didn't get far before he was whacked across the back of his neck with a pool cue. It then seemed they were gone almost as quickly as they had appeared. The majority of the crowd returned to the bar, disappointed there hadn't been more of a donnybrook. Blathers said, "Duff, will you wait here with Maggie for a moment? I need to go back inside and thank the boys."

While we waited, I could hear a cheer as it was announced that Blathers was buying a drink for the house. He was back in a minute or two. "Sure, they'll be sending me one heck of a bill for this one, won't they."

Chapter 46

Days went past without further incident until the first Saturday in April. It was time to collect the rents. It was a warm day for early spring, around sixty-five degrees. Just before ten a.m., Blathers and I came out of the entrance to the Third Avenue Elevated at 84th Street. Even though it was an unusually balmy spring morning, we both were wearing heavy topcoats. We each looked like we had put on an extra ten pounds overnight. Frieda said she couldn't make us look any better.

In the lobby of Blathers' apartment building, we sat on two chairs for the whole of the regular time, ten a.m. to noon. No one stopped to pay their rent. No one stopped to complain. No one even passed through the lobby. I asked, "Blathers, do you think this is strange?"

"Sure, I suspect that we are being boycotted, as they say. Let's go see if Stan is around, why don't we."

We went down to the basement. The door to Stan's rooms was open. Blathers poked his head in and then stepped back quickly. Someone came out of the darkness, and for a moment all I saw was a gun.

Blathers regained his footing and said, "Well, well, if it isn't Mr. O'Hara, of all people. Was it you, now, that was in that gangster movie I saw last week, or was it really Cagney? I'll bet you see all his movies so you know how to act like a real tough guy."

"Never mind the crap. The two of you don't move."

"Sure, now, Mr. O'Hara, I thought you were working for Grover Whalen."

"I freelance. I work for anyone who can pay the tab. The tab is a sizeable one for the likes of you two. You have made some folks very upset."

"So who were you working for when you killed Mr. Goldman?"

"What makes you think that was my job?"

"Because I think that it was you who tried to shoot Mrs. Goldman and shot Albert, your driver, instead. Good show trying to make sure there wouldn't be any witnesses. It was clever of you to have a car parked on the next street."

A smile flashed across O'Hara's face. "I think you'll find out soon enough that I'm no amateur."

Blathers continued to press the point. "So then you admit it was you who murdered jeweler Goldman and that fool Albert. I know you were working for Fritz Kuhn, because he tried to get me to do the job on Mrs. Goldman. I suspect you also did Harold Berger, didn't you?"

"Oh, Harold Stern? The shmuck at the construction site? Imagine faking the autograph of Hitler. So his name was Harold Berger, was it? I didn't know. Well now I know, and I know that you know too much. This is like getting a double payment. I'm going to get a nice fat fee for this, and I'm also going to get rid of a couple of wise guys at the same time."

I said, "Come on, be real, O'Hara. You're not going to shoot us here, with an apartment building full of witnesses."

"Did you see any witnesses this morning? Apparently, the Bund is throwing an all-you-can-eat-and-drink picnic today, to celebrate the lovely spring weather, you know, or maybe to celebrate the fact that this building won't have any, shall we say, *undesirable* tenants. All the current tenants have been invited. Now, it may be a beautiful spring-like day, but the temperature will go down tonight, and there will have to be a fire in the furnace. Pick up that shovel and throw some coal in there. There is a bit of a glow from last night's fire, and Stan has gone off to the picnic. We'll help him out, and maybe add something more to the fuel. By the way, Blathers, who will inherit your building? I hope it will be someone with a better sense of the way things should be done than you have."

Blathers shook his head. "Did you not hear of the Black folks that want to move in? Perhaps they'll inherit the building."

"If they do, they'll face the same fate as you and your pal here, and I'll earn another generous fee."

The door behind us banged open, and Maggie stepped in, waving her Saturday night special. "Not if I have anything to say about it. Drop your gun."

I knew this wasn't going to end well. She was standing too close to him. He spun around before she could move and snatched the gun out of her hand. Then he pushed her against the wall. "Well, a new twist, but I probably can use this to my advantage. I won't need the furnace. What will the cops find, do you think? Two men who were shot by this cute little gun, and the distraught woman killer who committed suicide. Let's get this over with." O'Hara pointed Maggie's gun at Blathers' chest and pulled the trigger.

Chapter 47

Maggie screamed.

Blathers fell back against the coal bin, shook his head, and threw a left hook at O'Hara's astonished face.

Maggie said, "Oh, my God," and hit O'Hara on the back of the head with the coal shovel.

Blathers ran his hand over his chest, picked something out of the fabric of his coat, and dropped it to the floor. "It's still hot."

Maggie said, "Oh, my God, oh, my God, Blathers why aren't you dead?"

"It's dead you would like to see me, now, is it?"

"Oh, no, no, but you were shot. You should be bleeding, at least."

"Now, Maggie girl, take a look at me. Do I look a little fat to you, and is it not strange that I'm wearing this heavy coat on such a lovely day as today? It's the latest thing, darling, body armor. See there, Duff is made up the same way, but, sure, it was lovely of you to be here to save our lives. We're much obliged for your help. Give me a good hug, now."

Maggie had some difficulty getting her arms around Blathers and his body armor, but she finally made it. While Blathers and Maggie held each other, and tears rolled down the girl's cheeks, I went into Stan's room to search for a phone. Surprisingly, there was one, probably so the tenants could call him when they needed something. "Operator, please connect me with police headquarters. I need to report an attempted murder."

Higgins was on the scene within the hour. O'Hara was still alive, but dizzy, and bleeding from the back of his scalp. Before he came to, we had him tied up with some rope we found in Stan's room. When Higgins arrived, O'Hara was still not sure what had hit him. That Maggie girl was stronger than anyone imagined. We explained what had happened. Higgins looked at the gun lying on the floor, picked it up, and held it out in front of him. "Is this the gun, then? It's no wonder your body armor worked so well. It'd be tough to put a hole in a tin can with this. Damn lucky he didn't fire the Luger at you." Two uniformed men came in as O'Hara regained full consciousness. The two cops handcuffed him, and Higgins announced, "Mr. O'Hara, you are being arrested for attempted murder and other charges which may follow."

Blathers said, "What about that guy Albert? I saw O'Hara shoot that poor fellow."

Higgins said, "That will be part of the other charges, but I think the FBI might be interested. I think they could try him for treason because he has been operating as an agent of a foreign country. There is a new law, called the Voorhis Act, that might be applicable. Hoover might not want to do anything about it, but it might be a good thing if President Roosevelt gets involved."

****

Saturday April 6, 1940
Dear Diary,
What an exciting day. What a scary day. What a

happy day. First, I followed Blathers and Duff to the building that Blathers is supposed to own in Manhattan. I have been cut out of things since I protested so much about using Blathers as bait to catch a killer. My father used to take me fishing when I visited him in Ithaca. They have a nice big lake there. So I know that when you put a worm on a hook to catch a fish, the worm gets eaten. When you use a man to catch a killer, the man stands a good chance of being killed. I didn't want Blathers to be killed.

Well, I knew he and Duff were going to the building today to collect rents. I also knew there was trouble brewing. None of the tenants had sent their April rent in like they did last month. I also knew that if Blathers knew I was there he would send me home, so I snuck around the building until I found the back door. I no sooner got in hiding in the basement than I heard someone else come in the back way. I didn't get a good look at him because of the bad lighting, but he went into the Super's room, so I thought it must be the Super. I had heard Blathers and Duff talk about him. I think his name is Stan.

After a little while Blathers and Duff came down the stairs and looked in the room. That was the exciting part. The guy I thought was the Super came out and pointed a gun at them. The reason that was the exciting part was because I had my gun with me. Just like in the movies, I got the drop on the guy.

Unfortunately he was too fast for me, and he took my gun away. Then he shot Blathers with it. That was the scary part.

But Blathers wasn't hurt. He was wearing... I think you call it a bulletproof vest. Blathers punched the bad guy in the nose, and I smacked him on the head with a shovel. They tied him up, and Blathers gave me a hug and a kiss. That was the happy part, the very happy part.

Book Five: "A good deed in a naughty world"
Chapter 48

With the reopening of the Fair only about a month away, both Blathers and I had a busy couple of weeks. We thought we had the scheduling done, and then two folks called and said they had changed their mind and wouldn't be working for us. We understood. We were offering a temporary job, and they had found good permanent employment. After a long depression, a good solid job was a dream come true.

Another guy had an auto accident and was laid up for at least a month. And finally, one of the women, who had done a great job for us, reported that she just found out she was pregnant, and her husband didn't want her to work. This was a big problem. We needed some women. There were women cons out there, and we couldn't have them searched by men.

Two weeks of hard work, lots of overtime for Blathers and me, and we filled the gaps created by all except the pregnant lady. But then we got lucky and one of the other women working for us had a friend who had just gotten divorced. She needed a job, and our gal agreed to train her. By the end of the third week of preparation, everything was ready.

Blathers and I didn't bother trying to collect rents on the first Saturday in May. Mr. Littlefield wrote a letter to each tenant advising them their rent was past due and they were in danger of being evicted. We still didn't expect anyone would pay up.

The second Saturday in May, the Fair reopened for its second season. The opening would have been headline news except for the fact that, two days before the opening, Hitler invaded Holland, Belgium, and Luxembourg. His excuse was that he had information Germany was going to be attacked through those countries. At the same time, he opened hostilities in France. Europe was in trouble.

****

Sunday May 26. 1940

Dear Diary,

President Roosevelt gave a wonderful Fireside Talk to America tonight. I think the whole country was listening. First he explained how bad things were in Europe because of the fighting. He said many people had been forced from their homes. They had no place to live and no food. He said the Red Cross was trying to help, and folks who wanted to help should send money to their local Red Cross chapter. But then a very scary part. He explained what he had done to prepare the Army and Navy for war and what he was going to do to make us stronger. It sure looks like we are going to get involved in that war. From what the President said about how things are in Europe and what Frieda tells us about what is happening to the Jews, maybe we should get over there and straighten things out.

I wonder too about what happened to all those folks on the boat that was turned away. They were supposed to land in Cuba, but Cuba didn't want them. Then they tried to land in Miami, but the U.S. Government said the quota was full. Then Canada didn't want them either. They all had to go back to

Europe. With Hitler taking over Europe, I'll bet they are in serious trouble now. He blames all the problems in the world on Jews.

****

By the end of the month, the troubles in Europe notwithstanding, it was clear that everything at the Fair was running smoothly. That was when I brought out my easel. "Blathers, as I recall, there were two tasks on our list when last we got together with Frieda and Maggie. Now, with the news from Europe, the work of the group is even more urgent. I think we should get in touch with Frieda, and have her bring the list here for a lunch meeting, say, tomorrow. I'll have the burger joint in Flushing deliver burgers and fries for us all. I'll get iced tea for me and Frieda, and beer for you and Maggie. She will drink beer, won't she?"

Blathers answered, "Was me sainted mother a Catholic?"

****

Frieda got there about five minutes before noon, lugging our oversized pad of paper. The burger delivery guy pushed his bike through the back gate about five minutes after noon. We all settled in to eat. That kid must have peddled like crazy, because the burgers and fries were still nice and warm. I displayed the first page of the list from our last meeting, the one where Blathers was elected to be the bait to nab O'Hara, and Maggie got upset. It read:

OUR TASKS

1. Find out who is killing people, so that none of us get accused.

2. Find out how to best fund the organization without going to jail.

165

3. For (1) It appears that the killings were authorized by Kuhn.

4. We believe that the same person did both the killings.

5. If we nab the actual killer, we may be able to inhibit the Bund's ability to employ other assassins.

I said, "Well, we have accomplished our first task, and nobody is the worse for wear. Now let's talk about funding. Frieda, is it possible that from here on in you will get your funds, shall we say, more legally?"

Blathers asked, "Sure, now that you have a motel, will that be a legitimate business able to support the group?"

Frieda said, "The rooms will be rented on a nightly basis to any travelers. The income will help maintain the property, pay off the mortgage, and provide food and shelter for some of our group. The profit, if any, will support our main work."

Blathers asked, "What about the rooms in the basement?"

Frieda frowned at Blathers. "What rooms in the basement? There are no rooms in the basement."

"Frieda, I watched the construction, you know. There are rooms at either end of the basement that are not able to be reached except by an outside door at each end of the building."

"Blathers, do you know how hard it is to get a visa to enter the U.S.? There are immigration laws, you know. People are afraid of letting too many immigrants into the country. They think they are going to have to support penniless Jews. They think all Jews are communists. They think too many Jews will destabilize society. I guess people either don't know that Hitler is sending Jews to prison camps where they will die, or else people don't give a damn as long as they are making a good living. But I care, and so some of the folks we help aren't here quite legally. Last year Robert Wagner sponsored a bill to allow twenty thousand Jewish children to come to the U.S. That could have saved the lives of twenty thousand children. Do you know what happened to that bill? Some powerful senator from the south kept it from getting to the floor for a vote, so it just died along with the twenty thousand children. That senator hated Jews so much he didn't care if twenty thousand children died. He apparently thought that only children from his state were worth keeping alive. Does that answer your question about the basement?"

"I didn't ask any question about the basement, now, did I? Sure, Duff, did you hear me ask about a basement?"

"The basement of what?"

Frieda smiled. "I'm sorry for the outburst, but people are losing their lives by the thousands every day. You know, perhaps my little tirade will also answer your concerns about our methods. It is as simple as this: for every law we obey, someone will die. To save lives, we need to bend the law a little bit."

Maggie said, "Not to change the subject but to get back to planning, what about the apartment building Blathers owns?"

Frieda said, "Thanks, Maggie. You are right. We need to focus on the business at hand. The building was more of a loan to us than a real transfer of ownership. It has been transferred back to the previous owner, a corporation owned by various folks who are, we'll just say, good friends of Mr. Littlefield. They're busy collecting the past-due rents as we speak."

I said, "So it appears the motel will not provide enough to do the job that needs to be done."

"That's correct. But my friends have been talking about another opportunity. We would like some time to develop the idea, and then maybe you will help us."

I said, "Sure, Frieda, you can count on me."

Maggie said, "I'm in."

Blathers said, "Sure, now, let me hear about the idea. Does it involve someone shooting at me again?"

Chapter 49

Several days passed. Several meetings were held.
Several options were discussed. After a week or so, on
Wednesday morning, when Blathers wouldn't be in
until noon at the earliest, and Maggie had gone off for a
coffee break, I made the call.

Two rings and, "Good morning, you have reached
Mr. Kunz's office. This is Ginger, his secretary."

Since Fritz Kuhn had become a jailbird, Gerhard
Kunz had taken over at the helm of the Bund. It was
said that most of the Bund members still considered
Kuhn the head even though he did steal their money. I
guess one of the ideas that Nazis held was that the
führer could do no wrong. Therefore, even if he did
embezzle the cash it wasn't wrong. I don't get it.

I said, "Good morning, Ginger. My name is Duff. I
am the Director of Security for the World's Fair. I
would like to make an appointment to meet with Mr.
Kunz. I will be in Manhattan late tomorrow. Would it
be possible for me to meet with Mr. Kunz at about half
past six tomorrow?"

"Will you hold the line for a moment? Mr. Duff,
you said?"

"That's correct."

"Hold, please."

It wasn't just a moment, more like five minutes.
"Mr. Duff, this is Gerhard Kunz. What is it that you

wished to see me about?"

"I think I have some information you can use. I also have an idea that I am sure will interest you, and I have been contacted by some people you may want to meet."

"Well, now, that's quite a few things. Okay, half six then, in my office. Please don't be late."

Blathers arrived at the Fair about one thirty in the afternoon. "You're early today, aren't you?"

"Sure, I came to see if I could take Maggie to lunch. Oh, gee whiz, don't worry now, we'll only be less than an hour. I'll be here till closing. Besides, it's not today, it's tomorrow that you usually go into the City, isn't it? Are you going to make your usual trip?"

"I am, yes. I have some business to attend to while I'm there."

"Well, I'll see you later, then, and best of luck with your business."

****

I left the Fair right at four on Thursday afternoon. Since my apartment on 41st Avenue is not that far from the rear entrance to the Fair, I walked home. As I do on my usual Thursday evenings, I showered and dressed more formally than I do for work. I walked around the corner and took the LIRR into Pennsylvania Station. I usually would have dinner at a little French restaurant in midtown, but this night I had business. I had phoned Henri at the Chez Marcelle earlier in the day to tell him that I would be in for dinner later than usual. He graciously agreed to hold my table.

Outside the train station, I hailed a cab. "178 East 85th Street, driver."

****

Ginger was still on duty when I arrived at the Bund office. She was just what I expected, statuesque, in a Wagnerian sort of way. I didn't really understand why men in power thought they had to adorn the front office with a woman whose main asset was the shape of her body. Maggie was cute, but her best asset was that she was smart. We could rely on her to make sound judgments when necessary—that was, in every case that didn't involve Blathers. When it came to Blathers, she was a little reckless. I guess I didn't really understand that either.

In any event, I was ushered into Kunz's room without delay. He sat there behind a large desk that must have originally belonged to Fritz Kuhn. "Please be seated, Mr. Duff. This is August Klaprrott." A second man was sitting in a stuffed chair by the window. "He and I are working together to carry on the great crusade of Fritz Kuhn after his unfortunate incarceration. Now tell us, what are your wonderful ideas, and who are the people who wish to meet us."

"I'll get right to the point. I believe I told your secretary that I'm in charge of security for the World's Fair. In this job, I meet many people from all parts of the globe. I have been approached by some visitors from Germany. They are not here in any official capacity. They are merely tourists, at least to all appearances. They wish to remain just tourists, but they have heard of you two men, and they would like to meet you. They asked if I could help them. Here I am."

Klaprrott eyed me suspiciously. "I see. Then, Mr. Duff, why is it you would take the time to get involved in this matter?"

"Well, sir, my current job will last for only a few

more months. I know the depression is over, but it is still difficult for a security specialist or private detective to find work. I need to, as you say, get involved in as much as I can where there might be an opportunity for some work. Who knows? If I can be of some help here, you might ask me to do some work for you in the future."

Klaprrott nodded, and Kunz said, "Well, do you know what it is these folks would like to talk to us about?"

"They were somewhat cozy about their mission, but they had a letter from someone in Germany, supposedly asking that they be treated with respect. I don't read German, so I'm not sure what it said, and I don't know who the person who wrote it is, but the stationery looked very, shall I say, official. What do you think? Do you think you want to talk to these guys or not?"

"You say 'these guys,' but you haven't given us enough to help us make a decision. Can you give us a good description of them?"

"It's two men. They both appear to be about forty years old. They are slender and look muscular, like they are athletes or are in the military. They each have a facial scar, which I am told is the official badge of Prussian army officers."

Klaprrott sneered, "Yah, already we are being characterized. Next there will be cartoons in the magazines showing what Nazis look like. Well, we will show them what real Nazis look like."

Kunz said, "August, these men may be the real thing. They may have been sent by Hitler himself. I think we must see them."

"Gerhard, we must be careful. You know there are strong factions in this country that do not hold our beliefs. Roosevelt is not our friend, and the Jews are very strong in America."

"Phooey, they were very strong in Germany. Now they are running for their lives. Our work here is to make Americans aware of the danger presented by the Jewish effort to control the world."

I jumped into the argument. "Maybe your work would be enhanced if you were in charge of some of the other organizations in the country doing the same work."

Klaprrott seemed to be interested. His eyes seemed to widen. "What do you mean? What other organizations are you talking about?"

"I don't really know. It is just that the two men who asked me to arrange a meeting with you seemed to think that a more unified effort to spread the Führer's ideas in the U.S. would be more effective."

Klaprrott said, "Did you say these men are from Germany?"

"That's what they told me. Of course, the only evidence I have is the letter they showed me. The also asked if I had any information about a guy named Pelly. Wasn't there a guy who ran for President by that name?"

"Yes, he is the founder of the Silver Shirts. August, we really must meet with these people."

I said, "How about next Thursday, same place, same time."

Klaprrott nodded. "Yes, that will be fine."

Chapter 50

Blathers arrived at the office at about 12:30. Apparently the lunch date with Maggie was becoming a regular thing. "Sure, and how did your business go last night?"

"Quite well, and I had a wonderful dinner at Chez Marcelle later. I'll tell you all about it when you get back from lunch."

"That will be lovely. See you then." The happy couple, if it wasn't too early to call them a couple, headed out the back entrance. I thought they were both eating too many hamburgers.

As I made myself a cup of tea and unwrapped the lettuce-and-tomato sandwich I'd brought from home, the phone rang. Since the half of the happy couple who answers the phone was out to lunch, I picked it up.

"Duff, this is Captain Fitzgerald. I need to meet with you and Blathers. Will you be there this afternoon? I would like to stop by between one-thirty and two."

"We should be here."

"I'll see you then." He hung up.

****

Blathers was as good as his word, and he had Maggie back from lunch by half-past one. I told him to hang around because Captain Fitz wanted to drop by and talk with us.

"Sure, he probably wants to congratulate us on

nabbing that murdering bastard O'Hara. It's a good show that he's off the street, isn't it, now."

As Blathers was gloating about our successful caper, Fitzgerald came in. "I have some news, and I thought it was best to tell you about it in person."

I said, "Don't tell me there has been another killing."

"Worse than that. O'Hara has been let go."

"What? What do you mean 'let go'?"

"The District Attorney said there wasn't enough evidence to prosecute him on any of the charges."

Blathers said, "What do you mean 'not enough evidence'? He confessed to all three murders right in front of us, didn't he, now?"

"He says he never did. He says you made that up. It's his word against yours."

"But there were three of us heard him admit it."

"He says the three of you are trying to frame him, to cover up the fact that your girlfriend tried to shoot you. There is no evidence that he even knew any of the victims he is accused of killing.

"His story is that he was there because he was looking for an apartment. He walked in just as Maggie shot you. Then someone hit him over the head with a shovel, and that was all he knew until the police arrived. He says the only hard evidence is that you were shot with a gun registered to Maggie, and that he was hit in the head. I keep saying that he said all this, but it was actually his lawyer. The lawyer is a hot shot and is threatening to sue the city for false arrest. The D.A. had no choice."

Blathers shook his head. "Me sainted mother always said that the wheels of justice grind exceedingly slow."

I said, "I'll call Frieda. Its back to item one on our list."

Chapter 51

It was a good thing we had so many of our staff from the prior year back with us, and the Fair was running smoothly, because our extracurricular activities were frustrating us beyond belief. O'Hara was back on the street, and Ginger from the Bund office called to change our appointment to a week later. She said Mr. Klaprrott had been called out of town. I wondered if O'Hara had got to those guys and blown the whistle on me. Blathers and Maggie, of course, knew about the plan, and I filled them in on my meeting with the new leaders of Nazi New York. The phone rang, and Maggie stepped out to answer in the other room. Then I asked Blathers if he thought our plan was in danger because O'Hara was on the street.

"Well, now, if you think about it, it's a huge possibility. Is there some way we can test that, do you think?"

"I called Frieda. She is coming here in the morning. Can you stop for your coffee, donut, and orange drink and be here by ten?"

"Faith, now, I'll tell you what I'll do. I'll have me a fine, leisurely breakfast of bacon and eggs, and real orange juice, and then I'll take the LIRR out here so as to be on hand at the appointed time without fail."

I said, "I understand there is a very good breakfast place in Maggie's neighborhood."

"I've heard that meself, but don't you know, I don't live in Maggie's neighborhood, do I, now."

We ended that conversation as Maggie returned from the other office. "No problem, just someone wanting to know what time the Fair closed. Strange that we got that call."

****

Everyone was on time for the morning meeting. Blathers said he took the Long Island Rail Road. "Sure, I took it home last night, as well. I went out the back and walked to Flushing so I could get a seat. You know, when the train stops at the main gate here, there's a mad rush for seats. If folks were smart, they would take the train east one stop to Flushing, and just turn around and ride to the City."

I said, "Gosh, Blathers, you are a clever fellow. Of course, if you were really smart you would live within walking distance of where you work, like I do. I save paying a fare, and I get some exercise as well."

"Sure, isn't that fine for you, but Flushing is too far away from Murphy's for me."

A little humor broke the seriousness of the occasion, and then I broke the news about O'Hara to Frieda. We discussed the possibility that, under the circumstances, our scheme might have been discovered by the Nazis. Frieda said, "It's the fact that the meeting was postponed that makes you suspicious, right?"

"Yeah, maybe it has no connection, or maybe it does."

"So it was Klaprrott who was unsure about having a meeting, and it is Klaprrott who is supposed to be out of town. Suppose we send our two men to the meeting on Thursday, like they were not informed the meeting was postponed. If Klaprrott is there, we will know there is something wrong. They will get out of there as quickly as possible, and we will be back to square one in all our plans. If Klaprrott isn't there and Kunz is, and it seems he is the most gullible, our boys can work on him and set things up for the following week. I am sure we will need to con both of them, and it will be easier if we do it one at a time."

****

It was a long day, and I was about ready to turn in when my phone rang. "Duff, this is Tony. You better get down here. All hell has broken loose."

"Isn't the Fair closed by now, Tony?"

"There has been a shooting. Fogarty is down, and Blathers has been wounded."

"I'll be right there."

I pulled on my trousers and grabbed a shirt from the closet. That time of night the fastest way to get to the Fair site from my place was to run there. I did the best I could.

****

Several police cars were on the scene. I met Tony at the security office. Blathers was sitting in a chair. An ambulance guy was applying a bandage to his right shoulder. "What has happened?"

"Ah, Duff, poor Fogarty is a goner, poor man. They have already put him in an ambulance, but this fella here says he won't make it to the hospital."

"A shame. How did this happen?"

"Fogarty and I were closing up. There was one last-minute drunk that we were going to keep overnight in the hoosegow. Fogarty was throwing him in behind the bars when all of a sudden the bastard seemed to

179

sober up. He pushed Fogarty to one side and took a shot at me. Faith now, wasn't me sainted mother looking down from heaven, and didn't she save me. I had bent over to pick up a used paper cup that someone had thrown down, and the bullet just grazed my shoulder. Fogarty went at the fella with his club, and the rat shot him, point blank, in the stomach. Then the fella took another shot at me, but I had dropped to the ground and rolled behind a garbage bin. I guess he figured I had a gun, so he took off out the back there."

As Blathers was finishing his story, Captain Fitzgerald came into the room. "Blathers, are you okay?"

"Sure, it's just a scratch, Captain."

"I came to tell you Fogarty was dead on arrival at Parsons Hospital. It was a very bad stomach wound. Do you know who his next of kin is?"

I said, "As far as I know, he has no one, Captain. That's why he didn't mind working at night. I'll check the files to see if he listed someone to be notified in an emergency."

"Well, if there's no wife or children, it can wait until tomorrow. Blathers, I'll have a car take you home. Duff, would you mind staying around for a bit? We have some people coming who will want to check out the scene, technical folks, you know."

I agreed to wait, and Captain Fitz waited with me. Within a quarter hour the place was swarming with folks scraping up blood samples, shooting pictures, and looking for fingerprints. That's how a murder scene is treated these days. As fast as all the technical people arrived, they left. Then Captain Fitz asked me to lock up and said, "Can you meet with the homicide people and me in the morning, say, ten o'clock?" I agreed, and as soon as I had the gates closed, I got a ride in the captain's car back to Flushing.

Chapter 52

In the newspapers the incident was in the headlines for one day. Then it quickly became back page stuff. There wasn't much room in the paper for local news, the way Hitler was behaving in Europe. Fogarty had listed someone to notify in the event of an emergency. It turned out he was a bartender in a beer joint on Roosevelt Avenue. I hadn't realized that Fogarty lived not far from me in Flushing. I was sure it was my responsibility to stop and see the fellow, but I was not at all comfortable going into taverns. I also knew that I was the person who needed to make arrangements for Fogarty's funeral. He was Irish. He was probably a Catholic, which gave me additional discomfort. I had never been in a Catholic church. I had never spoken to a priest. I had seen them around from time to time, in their funny collars.

I had finished meeting with New York's finest, who had made absolutely sure I knew what my duties were, and I was fussing about my predicament when Blathers arrived at the office. "I didn't expect you here today. You must not have been hurt that bad."

"Sure, it's just a little thing, except my jacket is a total loss. What's going on here?"

"Whalen ordered the Fair closed until five this afternoon, just to keep the thrill seekers away for a while. I met with the police, and now I have to go to a beer joint to tell a guy about Fogarty, and then I have to find a Catholic priest and arrange for his funeral."

Blathers got a look on his face that would embarrass the Cheshire Cat. "Well, gee whiz, you have to do what you have to do."

"I know, it's just that I don't really know how to behave with a bartender, not to mention a priest."

"Duff, do you want me to do these things for you?"

"Thank you for offering, but I am the one who has the responsibility. I can't avoid that."

"Then would you be feeling a little less apprehensive if I went along with you?"

"That would be wonderful."

"Let's go. We'll find the priest first. St Michael's is just up the street from where you live on 41st Avenue. The priest there will be very happy to bury a fine Irish gentleman like Fogarty."

We walked to Flushing, past my building. Blathers said, "So this is where you live, is it. It's a very nice building." At the end of the block, we found St. Michael's. "Sure, this church is so close to your place, you should be attending daily Mass." The Cheshire Cat was back.

Father Kennedy was very helpful. Once it was agreed that, since Fogarty was killed on the job, all the expenses would be paid out of Fair funds, making the arrangements was a piece of cake. Blathers seemed to know everything that needed to be addressed. For the type of service, Blathers insisted on a funeral mass. He set the day and time. He was sure that most of our folks would want to attend to honor Fogarty, so it would have to be before the Fair opened. He selected the appropriate hymns. "Amazing Grace" was not a choice.

It was much easier than I thought it would be.

Now we were headed to the next challenge.

****

Foley's Blackthorn Tavern was not more than a ten-minute walk from St Michael's. Apparently, this part of Queens was an Irish neighborhood. I had lived here for almost two years and didn't realize it. Foley, himself, was the man we were looking for. He was behind the bar when we arrived. Blathers was more comfortable here than he was with the priest. "Ah, Foley, I'm afraid we have some bad news regarding one of your customers."

"If it's Fogarty you be talking about, the news has already reached me. Who might you fellas be?"

We explained who we were and about the funeral arrangements. Foley put three glasses on the bar, reached on the back shelf, brought out a bottle of the finest, and poured three drinks. "To a fine Irish lad." He raised his glass, and Blathers raised his. I didn't know what to do. Foley and Blathers both poured down their drink. Blathers wiped his hand across his mouth. "Oh, I'm sorry, Foley. I didn't tell you that Duff here doesn't partake of the creature. If it's okay with you." Foley nodded and poured himself another. Blathers picked up my glass. Foley said, "A parting glass." Both drinks disappeared. By the time Foley made a sign with the information about the funeral, and a few more details were settled, it was necessary for me to put Blathers in a cab and send him home. The expenses connected with Fogarty's death were piling up.

The attack on Blathers and the murder of Fogarty was reassurance that we needed to give more attention to our first task. But we also needed to proceed with our plan to complete our second task, which was, in plain English, to cheat someone out of a large chunk of cash.

****

On the next Thursday I phoned Henri again. "My friend, this week I again have a special request."

"Ah, *monsieur*, anything that I can do for you, Henri is ready." I asked that he have a table for four, sometime between seven and eight. "It is no problem, *mon bon ami*."

Blathers and I set out for the Upper East Side around five. When we got to the Bund office on East 85th, we avoided the doorman by going in the delivery entrance. We each had a cardboard box wrapped in brown paper. If we were stopped, we had a delivery to make. Fortunately, no one cared where we were going. We took the service elevator to the floor where Jews were not allowed. We were really lucky. There was a maintenance closet almost directly across from the white supremacy office. The maintenance folks wouldn't be in until after most of the offices were closed. We had a spot where we could act if needed.

At exactly six-thirty, the elevator door opened and two figures emerged. The costumes were great. Both men were dressed exactly the same. They had dark gray suits, darker gray raincoats, and lighter gray neckties. Black snap-brim hats topped off the outfits, but the things that made them look most like European Germans were the wire-rimmed eyeglasses with small round lenses.

They opened the door. We could hear them say with what I thought was an authentic German accent, "Goot evenink, miss. Ve are here to meet a Mr. Duff." With that the door closed, and we heard no more.

We waited. About ten minutes passed before the door opened again. "Ve are sorry about de mix-up. It vas nice to meet you, Mr. Kunz. Ve vill be happy to return next veek vhen your associate vill be here."

As the two passed by the closet, in a loud voice one of them said, "Mr. Klaprrott is in Chicago, but he is looking forward to our meeting next week." The accent was gone.

Dinner that evening included Blathers, the two fake Nazis, and me. At first, Henri was a little taken aback, but when the actors removed their hats, coats and wire-rimmed glasses, all was okay. It is amazing what a few items do to change one's looks. Henri was very excited when the actors joined him in a chorus of "La Marseillaise." The only setback to our celebration was that Blathers had no idea what any of the items on the menu were. Henri finally recommended a special item, not on the menu, Le Hamburger. That and a glass of red wine satisfied our Irish friend.

Chapter 53

Blathers and I tried to get together as often as possible to make sure the Fair was as safe and fun as it could be. It had been a regular thing that youth groups would visit. While school was still in session, classes from all levels of education came to learn and play. Part of our responsibility was to provide an escort for these groups. If it was a school trip, a teacher would accompany the group, and take charge of the education and discipline of the students. When schools closed for the summer, we would get scout troops and 4-H groups and the like. We decided to hire some teachers to accompany these groups, for both security and educational reasons. Today we had agreed to meet at two-thirty to review our teacher applicants for what we called the summer season. As had been his habit of late, Blathers showed up early to take Maggie to lunch. "You know, Blathers, there is a new Chinese restaurant that just opened on Main Street in Flushing."

"Ah, sure, Duff, neither Maggie or me are partial to tea, don't you know. Them Chinese places always want you to drink tea."

"Enjoy your burger."

"We'll be back in good time for our meeting."

****

When our office romance returned from lunch, they were both surprised to see two extra persons sitting in my office. Blathers said, "Oh, gee whiz, if isn't Brown and Kowalski all over again. Did you fellows pay to come in?"

Brown said, "Knock off the wisecracks and sit down. We're here on serious business."

"And now what can be your serious business this time?"

"Another murder."

"Another murder, now, is it. Did you find another body somewhere in Bayside?"

"We're talking about the murder of your man Fogarty. It seems that lately when there is violence, you're on the scene."

Kowalski took his turn to speak. "Yeah, and where there's smoke there's fire." Was that going to be his only contribution for the day?

Blathers stroked his chin as he does. "Now, Fogarty's death was an accident. The killer was after me."

"We read the police report."

"Then you know I was the intended victim."

"We think that's what the police say, but we have seen too many situations where you were involved. The information in the report is only what you told them. There are no witnesses to confirm that there was a shooter at all."

Blather interrupted, "Now, wait a minute, if you please. Tell me again why you were reviewing this particular police report. Do you look at every police report, or was there something about this one that caught your eye?"

"The name Blathers."

"And faith, how in the world did you come to find

out the name Blathers was in this report?"

Kowalski opened his mouth again. "Our guy told us."

"Your guy. And what guy was that? Do you have men who stand around in police stations, or does that mean you have spies in the New York City Police, and you're using them to pin something on me? What in the world have you got against me?"

Brown said, "Other than you're a wise ass, not enough to book you. But like Kowalski says in his own clever way, you always seem to be around somewhere when somebody gets killed. We know what the NYPD think, but we think you being a major player is something, and the cops who investigated all these killings were Fitzgerald and Higgins, probably buddies of yours from the old country."

This was the first time I had seen Blathers get his Irish up, as they say. "A fine lovely speech, but all your information is circumstantial. I think the two of you are running around our fair city looking at every death that occurs to see if there is any way I can be connected to it. You should be arrested for harassment, yourselves. You're both a couple of nitwits, don't you know. You better get off my back, or there will be more violence than you want."

Brown said, "We usually take threats seriously, but in this case we'll overlook your outburst. But remember, as my gifted partner would say, if the shoe fits, you should wear it. I could name all the times you have been involved in a police investigation, but it doesn't matter. We think this is more than murder."

"Well, now, I certainly hope so. Murder is such a mundane crime, don't you know. What the hell are you talking about? I haven't murdered anyone, and I haven't committed any other crime. I don't think you have any business following me."

Brown was getting more angry, and he couldn't keep his mouth shut. "How about being a commie and a spy and a traitor. Is that enough crimes for you? If I thought I could get away with it, I'd plug you right here, right now, you scum bag. You come here to live, all you slimy, drunken, shanty Irish, and then you don't like things the way they are, so you want to change them. If I had my way, I'd send you all back to starve to death. We don't want you here, get it?"

I had to assume that the Brown family had come to North America at the time of the Revolution, based on that tirade.

I said, "Now that we know how you really feel, get off the premises, and don't come back unless you have a warrant. You two are barred from the World's Fair, because you are not very fair to the world." I got up from my chair and lifted Brown out of his chair by the front of his three-piece suit coat, spun him around, and gave him the bum's rush to the door. Kowalski ran out the door by himself. They both left their hats behind.

Chapter 54

After the FBI incident, Blathers took two days to cool down. He visited Captain Fitzgerald on his own to see if he was aware of the activities of Brown and Kowalski. "Blathers, they were in here right after the incident and asked to look at the report. They said they were after a killer who might have been involved in the incident. I thought they were talking about O'Hara, not you, so I let them see the report."

'Well, now, they are certainly after me, and I would have to guess that Duff is also now on their list after he threw them out. You know, based on Brown's little speech, I think they are a couple of rogue agents and the FBI doesn't know what they are up to."

Fitzgerald said, "I have a few friends who might know something about these guys. Give me a few days. I'll see what I can find out."

It didn't take Fitzgerald a few days. Later that afternoon he called to tell us that Brown and Kowalski were on special assignment to track down a gang of con artists. "Apparently J. Edgar Hoover and your boss, Grover Whalen, are pals. Hoover wants to get the people who scammed Whalen before the Fair closes so they can cover up the amount Whalen lost to the gang."

My comment to Fitzgerald was, "If those two are the best the FBI has, the government is in trouble." My comment to Frieda the next time I saw her was, "Don't worry too much. Those guys have been working on the case for over a year now and haven't gotten anywhere." My comment to Blathers was, "We need to add another task to our list—How can we mislead Brown and Kowalski?"

****

Since we now had three big jobs on our hands, we needed to prioritize. Blathers said, "Sure, there's nothing we can do about the scam until next Thursday, and I don't have any idea what to do about O'Hara. I think we have to wait until he makes another move. All we can do is be careful. Now, in the matter of the lovely pair from the FBI, I think it will be great fun to get those unholy bastards running around like the chicken on Sunday morning, that me sainted mother was intending for a special Sunday dinner." Blathers had his own ways of expressing clichés.

I asked, "What do you have in mind?"

"I think the first thing will be for us to apologize."

"You want to apologize to them? They owe us, and particularly you, an apology."

"Here's what we do, now. We call them. I still have their card here somewhere. We say we are sorry for the way things ended. We know they have a job to do and we don't want to interfere. We shouldn't be telling them how to conduct their business. We realize they are professionals. Sure, they'll eat that up like duck eggs. Then we remind them that we were at least partly involved in the scam of Whalen. If they are still looking for those con artists, we may have a lead. Then, to top it off, we invite them to lunch at the burger joint."

Blathers had me laughing. "What then?"

"Oh, gee whiz, won't that be the lovely part. We'll feed them some leads. I heard that the whole bunch has moved to California."

"Okay, but you make the call to apologize. I would be laughing too hard."

"I'll call them right now. No laughing out loud while I'm on the phone."

Chapter 55

We held another conference with Frieda and Maggie. I brought out his list. It now looked like this:

OUR TASKS

1. Find out who is killing people, so that none of us get accused.

2. Find out how to best fund the organization without going to jail.

3. For (1) It appears that the killings were authorized by Kuhn.

4. We believe that the same person did both the killings.

5. Help Brown and Kowalski.

Frieda said, "What does that mean? Aren't those the two FBI guys who have been looking for us?"

Blathers laughed. "Sure, they are, but we're going to help them look in the wrong direction, are we not."

I explained that, rather than giving them reason to continue to get close to the truth, we were going to befriend them and get them to chase some red herrings. "Of course, Frieda, we're not as clever as you and your friends, so if you have any good ideas of how we can get them to, as Blathers says, look in California, let us know. We are buying them lunch tomorrow, so think fast."

****

Brown and Kowalski were a little late for our lunch

get-together. They got off the LIRR at the Fair instead of Flushing and had to walk to the burger place. Blathers and I were such good customers there we were given the best table and told to stay as long as we wanted. When the FBI showed up, we stood and shook hands. Everyone sat down. We ordered, and I said, "We are really sorry about our last meeting. I want to assure you that nothing like that will happen again."

Brown said, "Look, we have a job to do. We aren't picking on anyone, but we need to get it done right."

Blathers said, "Now, don't we understand that. It's just last time my Irish temper got the best of me. When we started to think things over, Duff said that we should not be fighting against the FBI. We should be fighting to help them. So didn't we call, and aren't we here now."

Brown said, "Okay, so how do you think you can help?"

Kowalski still hadn't opened his mouth when the food arrived at the table. I was wondering if he would be able to open it to eat his burger. I took a bite and answered Brown. "You remember when we found the body at the Fair. Well, we were told not to do any investigating, but we are, after all, investigators, so we did some investigating. We think we found out things that you should know."

Kowalski was able to open his mouth to chomp out a big chunk of burger. He had a mouth full, so naturally that was the time he selected to say something. "Okay, then spill it." What spilled was catsup down the front of his shirt.

"We are not quite prepared to tell you anything today. But if you are willing to have us work with you, we will put together some information and suggest several possible avenues of inquiry."

Brown said, "That sounds good. When can we expect to hear from you again?"

"Give us a few days to think it through, and we will be in touch." Lunch ended. I paid the bill, and we all walked back to the Fair together, bosom buddies.

****

Frieda stopped by later that afternoon. 'I want to talk to both of you about the FBI guys. We have some ideas, but we need to know a little more about them. What are they like, smart or gullible? Do they have any character flaws you've noticed? That kind of stuff.

I said, "Well, I think Kowalski isn't too bright, but he must have some smarts, to get the job."

Frieda said, "Or know somebody with enough pull to get him in."

"That's possible. About Brown, it seems he is a first-class bigot. He's one of those America-for-Americans guys. Anybody who didn't come over on the Mayflower isn't welcome. I wonder how he gets along with Kowalski."

Frieda said, "Maybe he doesn't, and maybe that's the weak spot we're looking for. Let us think about it a little more. By the way, tonight is the meeting with the Bund guys. Have you been invited, Duff?"

"I'll be there. I'm not sure if I'm expected, but I'm going anyway."

Chapter 56

I was at the Bund office about ten minutes before the appointed time. I wanted to be sure I was a part of the evening. Right on time, our Nazis showed up, a testament to German precision. They had already met Kunz, and I introduced them to Klaprrott. The names they were using were Herman Schmidt and Conrad Zimmerman. They sat and adjusted their round wire-rimmed eyeglasses.

Kunz said, "So, gentlemen, Mr. Duff here says you have some interesting ideas for us."

Zimmerman reached into his inside jacket pocket. "Verst, ve vish to show to you our letter, zo you vill know just who ve are." A very official-looking letter was passed to Klaprrott. It was an attempt on the part of the con men to flatter Klaprrott by making it seem that they were sure he was in charge. Klaprrott passed the letter to Kunz saying, "Heil Hitler!"

Kunz put the letter down on the desk in front of him, and Herman and Conrad joined in a "Heil Hitler."

Then Herman Schmidt removed his glasses, took a handkerchief from his pocket, and cleaned the lenses. He replaced the glasses, carefully wrapping the wire temples around each ear. He looked at Klaprrott, once again bestowing the idea that he knew Klaprrott was the boss. "I make zee assumption zat you know who Villiam Dudley Pelley iss."

Kunz answered, "We know of him, yes, the Silver Shirts. What about him?"

Schmidt went on to explain how certain people in Europe were concerned that there were so many different organizations vying to become the leaders of Hitler's movement in America. "Zis man Pelley vould like to be zee Führer in this country. Certain people do not like zat." He continued explaining that the German leaders could not openly attack Pelley, but they could encourage their good friends in New York to make an effort to absorb Pelley's organization. "Ve haff been sent to arrange zat for you."

The co-leaders of the Bund glowed and nodded. Kunz said, "We like that idea. What do you need from us?'

"Fifty thousand dollars."

Klaprrott gulped. "Fifty thousand dollars! What for?"

Conrad Zimmerman stood up, reached over to Kunz's desk, and picked up his letter of introduction. "Zere vill be expenses. Germany is not able to provide funding for political reasons, zat I am sure you understand. If you do not haff de funds, zen ve shall haff to make ouder arrangements."

Kunz said, "Now, wait a second. We are just surprised, I guess, at the amount."

"Zee amount vas set very carefully. Ve haff living expenses. Dere will be costs to ensure dat ve haff support in Pelley's group. Dere might be some, how vould say it, liquidation costs. Ve need fifty thousand dollars in cash tonight. Do you haff the funds or don't you?"

"You need cash and you need it right away?"

"Zat iss correct. Ve are already a veek late in our plan because you vere too busy to meet vith us. I also do not tink dat you understand how delicate dis plan iss."

Kunz looked to Klaprrott for an answer. Schmidt smiled at Klaprrott. Maybe the message there was that he wouldn't believe them if they said they didn't have the cash. Zimmerman folded the letter in his hands and slipped it into his pocket to indicate he was prepared to leave. I sat back with my arms folded across my chest.

Klaprrott said, "We have it."

Schmidt said, "Goot. Give it to us now, and in two weeks the Silver Shirts vill be yours, and Pelley vill be no more."

Kunz went to the closet and pulled out a large shopping bag. Klaprrott followed him, jerked a piece of plywood off the back wall of the same closet, and opened a wall safe. The bag was carefully packed by the two Bund leaders while Schmidt and Zimmerman sat quietly. There was no need for them to do otherwise. They knew that neither Kunz nor Klaprrott would dare to put less than $50,000 in the bag. I just sat there, surprised they hadn't asked me to leave before the cash appeared.

The counting and packing took about five minutes. Before he handed the bag to the two phony representatives of the Third Reich, Klaprrott asked, "How or where can we reach you?'

"Ve are at the Algonquin, but ve vill be back to you zoon."

The men walked out the door with the bag. I tagged along behind. The three of us took a cab to Penn Station. Wire-rimmed glasses and gray neckties, along with two black hats, were deposited in the trash. We jumped on the LIRR North Shore line, and I accompanied two ordinary men off the train in Bayside. One was carrying a bag of groceries, and I had two gray raincoats, folded carefully so they looked like one coat, draped over my arm.

Chapter 57

While I was helping deliver the loot, it seems Blathers was busy. On Friday, he came to the office about half past twelve. He had another burger date with Maggie. "Ah, Duff, now, how did it go last night?"

"Frieda is busy hiding fifty thousand dollars in every nook and cranny of the motel."

Blathers literally jumped for joy. He grabbed me around the waist and gave me a big hug. "They actually coughed up the cash, now, did they. Isn't it a grand success."

"Yes! Frieda's guys were terrific. They are great actors and better con men. It was only a matter of minutes until they had those two Nazis packing a paper bag full of cash. And were they cool. They sat quietly and watched like someone was packing their lunch."

"That's wonderful. Now I'll tell you about my evening. Around seven, our new best friends Brown and Kowalski showed up."

"What did they want?"

'They said they were being pressured by their boss to get some results, and they needed to know what we knew about the gang they were after. I told them we thought that some of them were out-of-work actors, but we didn't want to say anything yet because you and I disagreed on some things. They wanted to know what things, so I told them I think they have all gone to

California, but you didn't agree."

"How did that work?'

"Well, now, of course, they wanted to know why in the world I thought that, so didn't I tell them. I said first that there are more jobs in California for actors, what with the movies and all. I said look at the success of *Gone with the Wind* and *The Wizard of Oz*. Why, don't you know, they are even talking about a Green Hornet movie. Then I said for number two, there's a big fair in San Francisco. We sent all our pickpockets and con men out there. They treat them better than we do."

"Have they left for California?"

"They are thinking about it. I'll bet we hear from them again soon. I think we should have them buy us lunch before we tell them anything more."

****

Later that day, Frieda called. She wanted to have a conference the next morning. Blathers talked to her. "Oh, gee whiz, Frieda, tomorrow is Maggie's day off. Can we make it for Monday, say, at about ten. Maggie girl really needs a day to herself."

Frieda agreed, and on Monday, she brought the large pad of paper with our list on it.

She said, "First of all, I want to thank all of you for your help. Fifty thousand dollars will save many lives. By the way, what happened to the glasses and hats? We're thinking of having Schmidt and Zimmerman call on Mr. Pelley. They will tell him how the Bund is plotting against him and for fifty thousand dollars they can disrupt their activity and get him an interview with Hitler."

I said, "The hats and glasses are in the trash at Penn Station, but I'll bet you can afford to buy new ones."

"Every dollar counts."

"Well, I didn't want to provide any trail that Kunz and Klaprrott could follow. Some German-looking guys were seen entering Penn Station, but they were never seen leaving."

Frieda laughed. "Duff, we are going to make a good con man out of you yet."

Maggie said, "There is one thing, Frieda. When the Bund guys finally figure out they've been had, they will come looking for Duff."

I said, "You are right, Maggie. That's one of the loose ends, but it's not the only one. Set up that pad, and we can list the problems we still face."

The easel was brought out and the paper was put in place. I went over and ripped off the sheet that was already written on. I crumpled it up and tossed it in the wastebasket. On the new page I wrote:

1. O'Hara is FREE.

2. Blather has been shot at and Fogarty murdered.

3. K&K will soon find out they have been conned.

4. Duff is their only lead. They will be after him.

5. Brown and Kowalski are still around.

6. They will be distracted by California for only a while.

Blathers was stroking his chin. I didn't say anything, and the ladies remained silent. It was only a minute or two and the stroking stopped. Blathers looked up and said, "As me sainted mother would say, we should fight fire with fire."

****

Our conference went on. Frieda was a natural con person. She knew all the tricks. "I went to college and studied acting and psychology. One thing I found out was that everyone has an idea of what he is like. I think we can play the strong egos of the Bund leaders against the seemingly poor self-images presented by Brown and Kowalski."

I remembered how the fake Nazis played to Klaprrott in the meeting. They rightly recognized that he would have to approve the expense of $50,000 before it could happen, and that if he approved it Kunz wouldn't dare disagree. They also saw that Klaprrott was, as they say, hungry for power.

Blathers said, 'Now, isn't that what I mean by fighting fire with fire. The Bund is one fire and the FBI is another fire. We'll get the FBI after the Bund and the Bund will be so busy they won't have time to bother us."

Under Frieda's tutelage we made plans and set them in motion. Blathers made a call to Kowalski and invited him to supper at, of all places, Foley's Blackthorn Tavern. Kowalski wanted to know if he should bring Brown along. "Why, sure, if he's the type of lad to enjoy a pint or two, by all means."

I called the Bund office. "Hi, is this Ginger?"

"Yes, it is."

"Hi, Ginger, this is Duff, you know from the World's Fair. Is Mr. Klaprrott in?"

"No, he isn't, Mr. Duff, but Mr. Kunz is. Would you like to talk to him?"

"Well, do you know when Mr. Klaprrott will be in?"

"I'm not quite sure. I'm certain, though, that Mr. Kunz would be happy to talk to you."

"Ah, well, okay."

"Hold one minute."

"Duff, this is Kunz. What can I do for you?"

"Ah, hi, Gerhard. I was just calling to see if you or Mr. Klaprrott knew a couple of FBI guys by the names of Brown and Kowalski."

"Brown and Kowalski? I think I have heard the names, but I don't believe I have ever met the men. I will ask August the next time I see him if he knows them, and get back to you."

"That will be great, Gerhard. Is Mr. Klaprrott out of town again?"

"Yes, he is. I'll get back to you." Click!

Frieda had been listening to both of our calls. When I hung up, she applauded. "Both of you are quick learners. Kowalski must be in seventh heaven, and Kunz is fuming. If Blathers hints to his dinner guests that Kunz is possibly the leader of the confidence group, and Gerhard complains to Mr. Klaprrott, things might get very interesting."

****.

Monday, July 1, 1940

Dear Diary,

Well, Frieda has been around the office quite a bit lately. Today we had another conference, and she was there, tutoring Blathers and Duff on how to be con men. The thing is, I have been a bit jealous of her in the past, as I thought she had her eyes on Blathers. Now I don't think so. She must have some boyfriend, but she never talks about one. The only man I have ever heard her talk about is the lawyer, Littlefield. Maybe he's her man.

It's obvious that Blathers and I have been seeing a lot of each other. It's not just the lunches at the burger joint. We often get together on the weekend, but we still haven't gone on what I would call a real date since Valentine's Day. I wish he would ask me to go out dancing sometime. Wouldn't it be super to go and dance to Benny Goodman!

Chapter 58

A good time was had by all at Foley's, according to Blathers. "Sure, didn't Brown miss the meal altogether. Kowalski and I put him in a cab after finding him slumped over the toilet in the men's room. It must have been something he had for lunch that didn't agree with him. Of course Kowalski was fine. Can't those Polish fellows drink, I'll tell you."

I asked, "How did the Irish make out?"

"Well, now, there was one fine Irishman who stood his ground. I know what and how to drink in establishments like Foley's. And I did make a new very best friend out of a certain FBI chap."

Maggie interrupted Blathers' story. "Duff, Mr. Kunz is on the phone for you."

"Thanks, Maggie. Hi, Gerhardt. What's up?"

"As I promised, I spoke to August, and he has never heard of either Brown or Kowalski."

"Thanks, Gerhard. "

"Yes, well, on another matter. As far as I know, we have not heard from your German friends."

"Well, it's only been a short time. You need to give them a chance to set things up."

"I checked at the Algonquin, and they are not registered there."

"Did you expect them to be? They are probably on their way to North Carolina."

"The hotel had no record of their ever being there."

"Thank God! When they told you where they were staying, I was afraid they had used their real names. You know there's a law against what they're doing. They could be hanged as spies. As a matter of fact, because you have done some business with them, you might be in the same boat."

"If that is so, what about you?"

"Me? I didn't get a dime out of this deal. It's between you and German spies." Click!

Now that that interruption was over, Blathers was able to continue his story. I said, "So what is your new best friend, Kowalski, up to?"

"Well, he's going to look into how Kunz and Klaprrott managed to get rid of Fritz Kuhn. I told him the information we have is that the two of them framed Kuhn in order to take control of the Bund, and now we have heard they are aiding spies. I told him that it sure would be a feather in his cap if he could prove they were cooperating with spies."

"What did he say about Brown?"

"After a few pints, didn't he admit he is bullied by Brown. I assured him that if he could bring down the Bund leaders, Brown would be put in his place."

'Well, let's hope they keep each other busy. That will allow us to concentrate on O'Hara."

Blathers shook his head. "I don't think I want to be shot at any more."

Chapter 59

It was business as usual for several weeks. Then Klaprrott called. "Duff, can I come to visit you?"

"Why, sure, Mr. Klaprrott. Will Gerhard be coming with you?"

"No. He is busy elsewhere."

"Okay, when can I expect you? I'll alert Security at the front gate. Just give them your name and someone will bring you to my office. "

"Would it be satisfactory if I came along within the hour?"

"That would be fine."

****

Klaprrott arrived about forty-five minutes later. "I am greatly concerned. It has been several weeks, and I have not heard from either Schmidt or Zimmerman. I have tried to trace them, but they don't seem to exist. Have you heard anything?"

"Holy cow, I haven't, but then I didn't expect to. I would think they would have been in touch with you by this time. Let me do a little investigating. I know some folks in Asheville. I can get in touch with them and see if they know anything from that end."

"That would be fine, but there is one other problem."

"What's that?"

"You mentioned the names of Brown and

Kowalski over the phone to Mr. Kunz the last time you talked with him. A Mr. Kowalski has been trying to make an appointment with me for some time now. Fortunately, I have not had time to see him. He says he is FBI. Do you know what he wants with me?"

'Gosh. I know him. Yeah, he's with the FBI. He and his partner have been doing some kind of investigating into a gang of confidence men. They thought they were operating here at the Fair. There was one woman who was playing a badger game in the Beer Garden, but we tossed her out. Anyway, I don't think that was who they were looking for. The gang they wanted played for bigger fish."

"Perhaps I should meet him. He might know something about Schmidt and Zimmerman."

"I don't see why not, but that's up to you. You don't have anything to hide, do you?"

"No, we don't, but I don't like the FBI. They say we have the constitutional right to say what we want, but then they try to say we are agents of a foreign government. They are two-faced and can't be trusted."

"Well, then, continue to avoid them."

"I will."

****

When Blathers came in later that afternoon, I told him about Klaprrott's visit. "Oh, gee whiz, I'd best get on the phone and pump up Kowalski." He dialed the FBI number. "Kowalski? Hi, it's Blathers. How are you doing with those German guys I told you about?" He paused to listen, then said, "Really! I wouldn't think a guy like you would let them get away with that. Gee whiz, you used to come in here all the time without an appointment. If Brown is scared to take them on, you

210

can take the bull by the horns and go get them by yourself."

"Okay, good luck, and let me know how you make out. You know Duff and I are both with you on this."

Blathers hung up. "We'll see how that works."

Chapter 60

Another month passed. We heard from the Bund. They were not doing well. As Hitler took over France and started on Great Britain, pressure built up against Nazi groups in the U.S. Kunz and Klaprrott weren't as charismatic as Fritz Kunz had been. Martin Dies and his Committee on Un-American Activities emboldened Kowalski to keep investigating the Bund. He discovered that there was $50,000 missing and unaccounted for. This led to the final downfall of the organization.

Toward the end of September, we had another call from Frieda. "I wanted to let you know that our good friends Schmidt and Zimmerman are back from North Carolina. It took them a while, but they promoted another $20,000 from Mr. Pelley and his Silver Shirts. Thanks to your help, with these funds, and the motel, we are going to become a legitimate charity. No more of this...I'll call it trickery. It sounds nicer. Oh, by the way, if you and Blathers are going to be around in December, you are invited to a wedding. Now that I am no longer a criminal, Hyman Littlefield has proposed to me. We are planning a wedding around the holidays."

I congratulated Frieda on all her good news and explained that things were winding down and the Fair would close for good next month. I was planning to return to Chicago and run my family's private detective agency. "I have asked Blathers to join me, but he is unsettled about what he will do. He's had some offers from relatives in Boston, but there is Maggie to consider."

"Well, you two and Maggie have an open invitation. If you can make it, just show up. And thank you all again for the many lives you have saved."

****

The fair closed on October 27th. I locked the gates for the last time and accompanied Blathers to the platform to take the IRT back to Manhattan. "It has been great to work with you, my friend."

"Thank you, Duff, It has been a lovely time working with you as well. You'll be heading off to Chicago, now, will you."

"I am. Business has been picking up. My father wants to retire, and he wants me to take over. He wants me to hire more operatives. Would you reconsider and come out there and work for us?"

"Oh, gee whiz, thanks for the offer, but as you know, some of my people have asked me to come to Boston. They are thinking of going into the security business there. And there is also Maggie. I want to see what might happen there."

As the train came roaring out of the tunnel from Flushing, I grabbed Blathers' hand. "I understand, and good luck."

We shook hands, and when Blathers turned to look for the train, I saw a hand reach out and push him toward the track. He was stumbling, unable to regain his balance, and it looked like he would fall in front of the train. I grabbed for his coat and pulled him back to safety. I turned and there he was—"O'Hara!"

Blathers saw him too. O'Hara threw a punch at Blathers. He blocked it and quickly pasted three short jabs on the assassin's nose. O'Hara took another swing at Blathers and missed, just as the train stopped and the doors opened. The wild punch carried O'Hara into the open car. He started back out of the train toward Blathers, fumbling in his coat for what I thought was his gun. The doors of the train closed behind him, but his coat was caught in the door. The train pulled out of the station and O'Hara became part of the platform wall.

Then the train backed up. What was left of O'Hara fell onto the platform floor. We were stunned. Captain Fitz came and arranged police cars to take us wherever we wanted to go.

****

Saturday, October 27, 1940
Dear Diary,
Blathers is here. He needs a lot of TLC.
Goodnight!

A word from the author...

I am retired from forty-five years in business as an insurance underwriter, agent/broker, consultant, and educator.

Upon retirement, I took up writing. I have attended many courses and workshops including the Colgate Writers Conference on four occasions.

I have two adult daughters, and live with my wife of 39 years, Kathe. No pets.